Joe,

I0538844

Bubbles

and

Buttons

A Novella

Benjamin J. Patterson

JOE, BUBBLES & BUTTONS

Copyright © 2015 Benjamin J. Patterson

All rights reserved. No part of this book may be reproduced or transmitted in any form or by any means, electronic or mechanical, including photocopying, recording, or by any information storage and retrieval system, without permission in writing from the publisher. All questions and/or request are to be submitted to: 134 Andrew Drive, Reidsville NC, 27320.

To the best of said publishers knowledge, this is an original manuscript and is the sole property of the author **BENJAMIN J. PATTERSON.**

Printed in the United States of America

ISBN-13:978-0692388853
ISBN-10:0692388850

Printed by Createspace 2015
Published by BlaqRayn Publishing Plus 2015

Prologue

Uughh.... What the hell happened? " Joe mumbled as he slowly opened his eyes and struggled to regain his senses.

As Joe became aware of his situation, he realized he was in a strange room bound to a chair with ropes and completely naked. Joe slowly surveyed the room in hopes of getting some clue as to where he was, how he ended up here and why he was here.

Due to Joe's position in the room, he was able to see out a window through a fold at the edge of the curtain. Joe struggled to focus his eyes on the outside environment until he saw a large red and green neon sign that read "**Outbound Motel**."

"Outbound Motel... how the fuck did I end up here!" Joe voiced.

From Joe's last memory, he had just left a diner in south Florida where he had been approached by two unknown women... then everything went black. *Maybe that encounter was the beginning of his journey to that motel or maybe that was some sort of dream sequence*, Joe thought, until the bathroom door opened.

As the door suddenly opened, Joe's dream sequence quickly became a real life situation with him now being face-to-face with one of the women from his memory and boy was she a sight for sore eyes.

Along with her too being completely naked, from her feet to her neck she was a lucky man's sexual delight but, unfortunately, her face, her only flaw, soured her voluptuous frame. She stood about six feet something and was thick in all the right places...thighs, hips, ass and beasts. Her face though, on the sour note, was covered by more craters than the surface of the moon. It was covered in multiple cuts, scars and bruises, evident of a violent life.

Besides her weathered face, the only thing preventing Joe from obtaining an immediate hard-on was uncertainty and fear of what had happened to him and what was ***about*** to happen to him.

"You finally awake, huh, mystery man", she asked Joe as she slowly approached him. "Now why exactly were you following us? "

Three years earlier...

The Florida State Maximum Security Correctional Institute was alive with activity as they prepared to receive the two most wanted criminals in the known world.. Bubbles and Buttons.

1

Introducing The Sexy and Sultry Bubbles and Buttons

Bubbles and Buttons were two highly promiscuous strippers working at the infamous **Bandits Strip Club** and they readily agreed to wild sex with club patrons as long as the price was right. Men would come from all corners of the globe to experience their boundless levels of sexual pleasure and their welcoming of violent deviant acts.

On this particular night, a Russian Mobster by the name of Marco made a visit to the club wanting to find out for himself if the rumors of the two were fabled or realistic. Marco was a six foot smooth faced Russian with solid black hair.

Bubbles and Buttons earned their names from the nature of their sexual exhibition. When the show started, all the lights in the club were turned out except for numerous multicolored strobe lights that flicked about the dark as cigarette smoke filled air. Shadows of two naked women emerged momentarily as a bubble bath filled tub rolled onto center stage; they quickly disappeared into the darkness.

A slow, sensuous song resonated through the speakers of the club as a bubble covered figure rose from beneath the waters, seductively starting her dance while she sponged herself down; completely captivating the audience.

Marco's eyes widened as he leaned

forward in his seat, watching intently as Bubbles gyrated and wiggled to the beat of the music. She then stepped out the tub, exposing her slim and sexy nude frame, causing instant erections in the crowd.

Bubbles slowly walked off stage onto the floor, approaching a table in front of the stage roped off from the rest of the audience like some sort of V.I.P section. Another woman sat at that table silent and still, anticipating Bubbles arrival.

The darkness of the club shrouded the woman's appearance until two of the strobes lights revealed her wearing a long, buttoned down trench coat. Bubbles moved to stand behind the woman and began to softly caress her body as she continued her routine. The mysterious woman stood, towering over Bubbles with a six foot frame, faced her.

Bubbles slowly unbuttoned the woman's trench coat to expose her naked, voluptuous, Amazonian frame as a voice suddenly came over the club's loudspeakers. ...

"GENTLEMAN I NOW INTRODUCE YOU TO THE SEXY AND SULTRY BUBBLES AND BUTTONS! "

The club lights in flashed on, giving the onlookers a better view of the show at hand. Buttons grabbed Bubbles by her waist and carefully hoisted her onto the table, laid her back and propped her legs on her shoulders drawing anticipation of some hot girl on girl action. Buttons then placed her hands on the inner thighs of

Bubbles and began eagerly lapping and munching on her soft spot.

"Mmm...." Bubbles purred in ecstasy as Buttons drove her tongue deep into her.

By this time, men in the club had pulled out, satisfying themselves to the erotic display.

Marco rose from his chair, making his way towards the women but was stopped at the ropes by two brawny bodyguards. He stepped back, reached into his pocket and pulled out a large roll of hundred dollar bills which instantly drew the attention of the performing women.

"Hold on Bruno, we want a private dance with this one," Bubbles said to one of the bodyguards. The two continued the exhibition for another few minutes before ending their show. Once they were finished, other strippers came out to entertain the rest of the crowd while Bruno escorted Bubbles, Buttons and Marco to a private area.

"So what's your pleasure stranger?" Bubbles asked as she and Buttons slowly undressed Marco.

Marco put the large wad of cash he took out of his pocket on a table in front of them along with another wad he took out of his other pocket.

"Ten thousand dollars and this is mere pennies," Marco said in a strong Russian accent.

Bubbles picked up the money her eyes locking like Buttons' on the wad as if they were in a state of hypnosis, huge smiles streaked across their faces.

"What do we have to do," Bubbles

eagerly asked.

"My name is Marco and I am a very wealthy and powerful international business man. My clientele and I earned our power through hard work and in return we play harder; especially when it comes to the physical pains and pleasures of life..."

"You will work for me and I will help you become stronger women so you will be able to fully fulfill the appetites of my clientele, but first I must see if your current skills are as I hear. "

"After we show you our current skills, you won't think anything needs any refinements.. let's take 'em to outer space Buttons" Bubbles said, raising Marco's shirt and biting Marco's burly. hairy chest, while Buttons pulled off his pants to lavishly stroke his dick.

"Suck me and fuck me you fuckin' dirty sluts!" Marco demanded in his strong Russian accent.

"Ooooh...I like that" Buttons said in a strong sexy voice as she lowered her mouth over Marco's now erect dick.

"Now you come here and let me taste your pussy," Marco demanded to Bubbles.

"Ooh you kinky" Bubbles responded, as she climbed over Buttons and into Marco's arms cautiously. "I hope you ain't gonna drop me..."

Marco interrupted her forcefully, "I didn't say speak did I? You do want the opportunity I'm offering yes," Marco sternly asked as he glared deeply into Bubbles' eyes. Bubbles then nodded her head yes.

"With my offer comes pleasure and pain, the pleasure can be endless but the pain begins with submission. "

Buttons obviously had no problem with Marco's offer because she continued to feast on Marco's rock hard nine inch rod.

Slurrrp.....slurrrp.....slurrrp..

Bubbles then released her fear, gripping Marco's shoulders tightly to signal to him she was ready and willing for him to taste her and her submission to him.

Marco then lifted Bubbles' moist pussy into his face, dug his nose into it and hungrily began gnawing at her clit, causing her to convulse and wiggle in his arms in pleasure.

"Damn muthafucka...you sure can eat some pussy," Bubbles said as she fed herself to Marco.

While Marco's face was buried knee deep in Bubbles' pussy, Buttons released her lip lock on his saliva soaked dick, pushed her large meaty ass against his stomach, slammed down on him and punched his nine inches deep into her. ..

"Uh-hmm..." she moaned in pleasure as she forcefully rode his dick.

As they fucked, Bruno, the bodyguard and another guy walked into the private room. Bruno himself stood about six feet tall and this guy slightly towered over him. He had a strong Italian accent and reeked of cheap cologne with a briskly beard on his face.

"Sorry for my intrusion but anytime anyone commands the attention of my two best ladies I feel obliged to introduce myself", the guy said as he lit a cigarette.

Joe, Bubbles and Buttons

Both Bubbles and Buttons' eyes fixed on him with a slight bit of fear as they ended their acts of pleasure, now paying attention only to this guy with Bruno.

Marco pulled his face from Bubbles' juicy pussy while still holding her in his arms with a look of contentment on his face...

"So who the fuck are you to interrupt me like this?!" Marco didn't like having his pleasures interfered with.

"You can call me Leo like the lion. I own this joint and these are my girls, so I feel I can interrupt whoever the fuck I want."

"You're just the man I wanted to see," Marco responded.

Marco then tossed Bubbles onto the sofa, brushed Buttons away from his swollen dick and reached for his clothes. He reached in his jacket pocket and pulled out a check book.

"I want these girls..." He nodded his head toward the two young women. "What's your price?"

"As you can see my friend, these girls are worth a lot to me and my establishment and to put a price on them would be almost impossible. If I were to even consider what I would be losing I would think no less than a million dollars. So if you don't have a million dollars I suggest you get the fuck out of my goddamn club right now" Leo demanded.

Bruno then raised up his shirt and pulled a silver .45 pistol from his waistband and pointed it at Marco.

"I came to do business with you and

this is how you treat me," Marco asked.

"If you came to do legitimate business no, but you, on the other hand, came to take my business and this is the treatment you receive... now get your ass up and get the hell out of my club!" Leo's patience had run out with this Russian prick. What fucking nerve!!!

Marco stood to place his check book back into his pocket.....

"Bruno,"   Leo said sharply .

Bruno quickly stepped closer to Marco, "Don't make any fast moves smart guy..."

"I'm just putting my checkbook away since my money is no good here.." Marco replied as he placed his check book in his jacket pocket.

In almost the same movement, Marco put his checkbook away and pulled a switchblade from the same pocket, slicing Bruno ' s jugular like a fish being filleted. It happened so quickly no one in the private room knew how to respond. They all just stared in shock as a small slit opened up in Bruno ' s throat and blood started pouring out as Bruno dropped to his knees and fell to the floor.

As Bruno's body fell to the floor, Marco grabbed the gun from his hand and calmly stated "no one move."

"You know what the fuck you just did you son-of-bitch, you just signed your death warrant" Leo barked.

"Please don't kill us sir we haven't seen anything and don't know anything, " Bubbles pleaded.

"Don't worry, you are the reason I'm here so I have no intentions on killing you ladies, but my friend Leo over there is another story..." He turned his attention to Leo... "I just came to do businesses with you and you had the audacity to threaten my life," Marco said as he aimed the. 45 pistol at Leo's head.

"If you touch one hair on my head the Italian mafia will be elbows deep in your ass before you can get to the parking lot" Leo barked.

"Well Leo, my friend, I guess there's only one thing I can say to that..."

BOOM!

Marco's last word to Leo was a bullet in his brain. Marco pulled the trigger and sent parts of Leo's gray matter all over everything in the private room including Bubbles and Buttons. With a look of satisfaction, Marco turned his attention back to Bubbles and Buttons ...

"Is our arrangement still good ladies?"

"We still good... shit...that muthafucka wasn't paying us right anyway, "Bubbles replied as Buttons started rummaging through poor dead Leo's pockets.

"This room is soundproofed so nobody heard us, but we better get the hell out of dodge before someone comes looking for him," Buttons added.

Bubbles and Buttons grabbed some clothes and Bubbles then led Buttons and Marco out a back door of the club. They all then quickly ran to Marco's car.

"What a fuckin' rush," Bubbles yelled out in excitement.

"So Mr. Marco... When you came here looking for us did you plan on killing Leo?" Buttons asked.

"I never planned on killing anyone but no way in hell will I allow any muthafucka to threaten my life," Marco harshly responded.

"I'm starving! Can we stop to get something to eat," Bubbles asked.

"We leave for Russia now... you can eat on the flight," Marco responded.

"What the fuck do you mean we leaving now?! What about our families and our lives here? You expect us to just up and leave everything," Bubbles asked.

"I am more than capable of replacing any material possessions. As for personal relationships, that is for you two to decide and decide it now," Marco demanded.

Bubbles and Buttons stared deeply into each other's eyes, silently communicating with each other on such a critical decision. Bubbles then pulled the money they received from Marco out of her purse and gave half to Buttons.

"Even though we can never go back to Bandits, we can always work any other place in the country but will we see money like this and we may now be wanted by every Italian mafia hit man in the city. I know I won't see money like this and we will always be able to come back home; especially if we make lots of fucking money, I'm going...what about you," Bubbles asked Buttons.

"We're a team and I'm not going to just sit here while yo ass makes all the damn money... I'm in too," Buttons replied.

"That's great news ladies! Now I won't have to kill you two," Marco said with a devilish grin on his face as he slowly un-cocked a silenced pistol on his lap. Both women eyed the pistol in Marco's lap...

"Were you really gonna to kill us?" Bubbles asked.

"Only if I had to but no need to worry...so just relax," Marco replied.

Marco drove to a private airfield where they all boarded a plane and took off for the wilds of Russia and the Iron Curtain.

2

Training Begins

When they landed in Russia they left the plane and Marco led them to an awaiting limousine.

"Damn it's cold here," Buttons said as she crossed her arms and rubbed them down to create friction to generate some heat.

"Don't worry, I have coats for you two in the car," Marco said.

They all climbed into the limo and it drove for a while over snow covered roads until they reached a large structure similar to the castles of medieval times.

"Holy shit... is this your place?" Bubbles asked as she and Buttons stared in awe with saucer-sized eyes at the tremendous dwelling.

"Yes, this is my home here in mother Russia but I have many more all around the world. "

They exited the car and Marco led them into the house. The inside of the amazing structure more than complimented the outside. Gold, wood grain and marble covered every noticeable inch of the place like something only dreamed about.

"Come follow me," Marco said.

He led the two women through a door that led down some stairs into a dark basement area.

"Where the hell are we Marco?" Bubbles asked. Marco moved away from the women slowly in the darkness.

CLICK!

Lights came on, illuminating the room..in one corner there were two beds, a sink, toilet, shower and even a kitchen set up; while on the other side of the room was a large cage.

"What the fuck is going on Marco!" Buttons angrily asked.

"I told you this deal comes with pleasure and pain.. you experienced some of the pleasure when we met, now it's time to get to the pain. While you two are in training, you will live down here and have to earn your way to living in the house by accepting and welcoming pain," Marco said with a devilish smirk on his face."

"Beside the fact that we are in a strange country and you possibly killing us, is there any benefit in us going through this so called training," Bubbles asked. For the first time since initially seeing Marco in the club, she was feeling qualms of fear tightened her gut.

"I will also pay you two one thousand dollars each for every day of training you survive," Marco responded.

"Every day we survive.. what the fuck is that suppose to mean!" Buttons exclaimed. This shit was getting crazier by the minute and they were trapped. Maybe they should have thought this through a little better!

"In my business I require only strong women, which I believe you two are. This type of training either eliminates the weak or makes the strong stronger. " The insanity they had previously missed was now shining brightly in Marco's eyes.

"And if we are not strong enough," Bubbles asked.

"Then you will die," Marco replied rather matter-of-factly.

"So when do this training begin," Bubbles asked.

"Your training begins tomorrow so I suggest you two get settled in, eat something and get some rest, " Marco said as he made his way toward the stairs. When he reached the top, he turned around to speak...

"Also if you violate my rules at any point, I will kill you and feed your carcasses to the wolves."

With that, Marco went through the door at the top of the steps.

———————————————

Joe, Bubbles and Buttons

Bubbles and Buttons toured their new home for their training period. They walked over to the cage in the room and noticed the ground was covered in what appeared to be blood stains.

"Is that blood all over the fucking ground," Buttons asked Bubbles.

"It sure does look like it but I'm not sure," Bubbles responded. She wasn't sure because being sure would mean they really had just descended into the basement of hell and might not live to come out!

They then went inside the cage to examine it more closely. As they looked the cage up and down, they saw a small, fresh puddle of blood with a couple of teeth lying in it.

"What the fuck?! We need to find out what the hell we really have gotten ourselves into," Bubbles said as she headed for the stairs.

Bubbles climbed the stairs to the door leading into the house. She turned the knob but it was locked so she banged on it furiously. After a few seconds, the door opened and there stood Marco was holding a pistol in his right hand.

"What the fuck is going on?" Marco asked.

"What the fuck is going on you ask! We should be asking you that damn question. There is blood and teeth all over that goddamn cage down there," Bubbles angrily voiced.

"Oh shit..." Marco grinned sadistically "...I apologize. I thought my guys cleaned the cage of all that. I will make sure it gets cleaned before your training starts tomorrow. Don't worry, a little blood and guts won't hurt you all. Now get some sleep because you would want to be well rested for tomorrow or that could be your blood and teeth on the ground. "

Marco then closed and locked the door sending Bubbles back into the basement where Buttons was waiting.

"What happened... What did he say," Buttons asked.

"Whatever this shit is, it's dangerous so the only way we are gonna to survive this is to stick together... You got me," Bubbles asked Buttons.

"Yeah I understand," Buttons responded. The women cleaned themselves up and huddled together in one bed as they drifted off to sleep.

Joe, Bubbles and Buttons

_____

The next morning, Buttons opened her eyes, looked over and saw the comforting sight of her best friend Bubbles huddled next to her. She kissed her in the forehead and sat up to stretch, being careful not to wake her still sleeping companion. After her stretch, she slowly surveyed the room with wide eyed shock, suddenly reminded of where she and her friend were.

"Bubbles... Bubbles... Wake up," Buttons said in an urgent whisper as she shook Bubbles awake.

"Damn girl... What the hell is wrong with you. I'm trying to get some sleep," Buttons mumbled.

"This is the first day of training," Buttons told her.

"Training? Training ...oh shit training!" Buttons said, as she popped upright in the bed, she too shocked and painfully reminded of where they were.

The silence was suddenly pierced by the sound of Marco's voice out of nowhere.

"Oh good, the two of you are finally awake. I hope you had a good night's rest because today we find out what you two are made of. I will be down with some breakfast and a change of clothes shortly," Marco said as his voice rang over some speakers embedded in the ceiling.

Minutes later they heard the door leading to the house unlock and open followed by footsteps coming down the stairs, but before they saw anyone they were overtaken by the smell of coffee and other aromas so good, their collective mouths began to water.

"Mmmm...it smells like breakfast is just about served" Bubbles said to Buttons with a huge smile spread across her face.

Just as she finished her sentence, Marco's feet appeared as he reached the bottom of the steps with a tray in his hands, but to their surprise, Marco is followed by a teenage boy carrying a stack of clothes.

When Marco and the teenager reached the bottom of the stairs, Marco spoke to the boy in Russian and the teenager laid the stack of clothes on the bed and went towards the cage at the other end of the room.

"Good morning ladies, let's eat and drink because today is the first day of the rest of your lives," Marco said with that same twisted gleam in his eyes. Marco poured the women coffee and handed them plates of food as the teenager started cleaning the cage.

"Damn Marco, what's the deal with treating us so good but making us stay in this fucking hole," Bubbles asked as she chewed and swallowed her food.

"The only reason you are staying down here is to ensure you stick to your training regiment ...there is no benefit for me to make your training completely unbearable," Marco said.

"Can we now at least know what we have gotten ourselves into," Bubbles asked.

Marco pondered the question for just a second before continuing...

"Well I guess it's about time I revealed

the rest of the puzzle. My friends and I organized a special club where we collect a select choice of sexual and ferocious women for a special sport of ours, we call you all **Gladiator Escorts**," his smile widened as he sipped his coffee.

"Gladiator Escort....what the hell does that mean? Sounds like some old freaky, crazy shit to me" Bubbles replied.

Marco glared at Bubbles, "I see you like to ask a lot of questions and your friend here seems to just go with the flow."

"We're a team. I am more of a talker and thinker and Buttons is more of a doer which is why we make such a good team. I make up our dance routines and Buttons is good at making it happen plus she has an ass and tits men and women drool over," Bubbles answered with a little heat. She was determined to show Marco no fear, although a part of her was scared out of her mind.

"Ok...Well, to put things simple, some jobs will require fucking and some will require fighting. Some of my clients enjoy watching women beat each other to death and others enjoy a tough submissive woman they can act out their deepest and darkest fantasies with. An act their significant others at home would never allow. You two will fulfill both of these needs and in turn you will be paid and treated very, very well." Marco explained the plan while pouring himself another cup of coffee. He was perfectly at ease with the insanity he had just described.

"Fantasies is what we do but I don't know about the fighting to the death part...ain't never tried that shit before" Bubbles said with worry in her voice. Now she understood exactly why her brain was screaming "get the hell out of here...NOW!"

Bubbles had more questions of course...

"And how many fights do you expect us to win?" Bubbles asked.

"I understand this business can really jeopardize one's health, so all I ask for is ten fights over ten weeks and you both will be set for life. During this time you will train down here for two weeks and *if* you survive, you can live in the house and move about as you please... "

"..I will provide you with all the training you need and the rest will be up to you" Marco responded, rising from the bed to leave the two to discuss their fate, although it was obvious all decisions had been made.

The teenager finished cleaning the cage and approached Marco, telling him something in Russian. Marco answered him hurriedly and the boy then collected the finished breakfast dishes, making his way back up the stairs

"I hope you enjoyed your breakfast because your training starts in mere minutes," Marco said as he looked towards the stairs...it was as if he was waiting for something or someone to magically appear.

A few seconds later there were footsteps coming down the stairs again; it was the teenage boy followed by two 'rough looking' women to use the term loosely. The teenager led one of the women into the cage and sat the other to the side. Both women were dressed in nothing more than rags with needle marks all over their bodies and they carried a nasty stench with them as they slid their feet across the cold basement floor.

"Whose first? Either you choose or I choose," Marco barked.

Bubbles and Buttons then turned facing each other, their silent communication conveying the madness of the whole thing, yet their inability to change the situation now. They were stuck and their only way out was to fight their way out...

"I'm going, " Buttons said in a serious tone. The die had been cast!

"She did say you were a doer...I like

the enthusiasm," Marco said as he walked towards the cage and gestured with his finger to Buttons for her to follow him. Marco then said something to the boy in Russian and the boy handed Marco a small leather case. When Bubbles reached Marco he placed his hand on her shoulder,

"You are quite a large and sexy woman.. if you want to win, use your size and strength along with using all your anger and pain in your life as fuel..."

Marco then went inside the cage and walked up to the woman slumped on the ground in a corner. He unzipped the leather case, pulling out a small vial with a clear liquid inside along with a syringe. He inserted the syringe into the top of the vial, carefully withdrawing a precise amount of the liquid, and injected it into the woman's neck. Marco then slowly and carefully put the vial and syringe away as he walked out of the cage.

"Enter the cage and go to the opposite end," Marco demanded Buttons.

Bubbles was right there on the outside end where Buttons was standing, holding her hand through the cage bars. ..

"Just be strong.. you can win this baby. I'll be right here, now go and kick that bitch's ass," Bubbles told Buttons.

They then exchanged smiles. ..

"She's waking.. it's time to get ready! " Marco barked as he closed and locked the cage.

———————————

The woman slowly stood up and locked her bloodshot eyes onto Buttons.

The woman slowly rolled and flexed her shoulders before she started screaming and rushed Buttons like a wild cat.

In an instant, Buttons side-stepped the woman, grabbed her and with her own momentum, slung her into the cage. Buttons then quickly scooted to the opposite end of the cage.

"You have her down, don't run, you have to strike now!" Marco yelled at Buttons.

Buttons looked over at Marco and before she could turn her head back around, she was tackled to the ground, now fiercely being clawed at by the drug crazed woman. She bent her head and bit Bubbles hard on her shoulder.

"Ahhhhh you bitch!" Bubbles yelled a blood curdling scream as the woman ripped a chunk of flesh from her shoulder.

"First blood...I love it," Marco said as he eagerly watched with that wicked smile on his face.

"FUCK HER UP BUTTONS....FUCK HER ASS UP!!!" Bubbles yelled from outside the cage as she excitedly jumped up and down almost like a kid watching a playground fight.

The woman then began to bang Buttons' head on the ground violently and forcefully. Buttons reached up with all her might, grabbed the woman firmly by the head, using her weight advantage to roll the woman over. Once on top, Buttons took her thumbs and forced them into the woman's eye sockets as they both yelled from the intensity of the fight. Buttons continued pressing until her thumbs sank into bloody spots in the woman's head and she just stopped yelling and fighting. It was over as fast and violently as it had begun.

It took Buttons a moment to realize the woman wasn't moving anymore. The adrenaline pumped through her veins like that drug had in the other woman's. She slowly removed her thumbs from the woman's eye sockets and rose to her feet breathing heavily.

"Yea baby... you did it," Bubbles yelled at Buttons.

Just as Buttons started walking towards the cage door she felt a tug at her ankles and to her surprise, the woman wasn't dead yet very close to it. She still had some fight left in her even though she was now completely blinded. With this woman now completely at her mercy and grabbing at her ankles, Buttons looked over at Bubbles and Marco with a look at confusion.

"What the fuck are you waiting for... finish her!" Marco screamed.

"Isn't this enough! The damned woman is blind as a bat at noon...what more can she do," Bubbles cried out.

Marco pulled a pistol from his waistband and pointed it back and forth at Bubbles and Buttons..

"I run a very serious business and I am a very serious man about my business so when I say finish her I expect you to do it or should I just kill you or your friend? Now what happens next is your decision... either she dies or one of you die!"

While they debated, the blind woman

made it to her feet and was now trying to feel her way to Buttons, still in attack mode. Buttons quietly stepped behind the woman, putting her in a vise-like choke hold. As the woman struggled and yelled to free herself, Buttons gave Marco a cold hard stare before she snapped the woman's neck.

"Is that what you wanted to see... you brutal bastard" Buttons asked as she walked towards the cage door.

"That is exactly what I wanted," Marco responded as he opened the cage door. "I hope you are prepared to fight or die," Marco said to them both.

He told the boy something in Russian and the boy quickly went inside the cage, hoisted the woman's dead body over his shoulder, carrying it away.

Joe, Bubbles and Buttons

As Buttons walked out the cage Bubbles walked in as she and Marco traded stares of contempt. Marco then shouted commands in Russian to the boy and he then led the other woman into the cage. Marco then went to the woman and injected her also with the liquid in the vial in the leather case.

"Should that kid really be here watching this shit Marco," Bubbles shouted. "You really are one twisted muthafucka!"

"Where the kid needs to be is the least of your concerns Bubbles... she's waking up..." Marco laughed, pointing towards the second woman as slammed the cage door shut.

Even though Buttons had it bad not knowing what was getting ready to happen to her, at that moment Bubbles had it worst because she knew what was coming and now the question was... Was she ready. Whatever Marco used on the women to make them fight had to be strong and fast. This woman was fired up and screaming just seconds after being something like the walking dead. Buttons wished Bubbles good luck and before Bubbles could part her lips to answer the woman was in full fury.

As soon as Marco said fight, Bubbles unexpectedly exploded onto the woman and drove her backwards to the back bars of the cage. Bubbles then gripped the woman's head between her hands and began to beat the back of her head on the bars. Whatever it was that Buttons unleashed overpowered Marco's magic potion because Bubbles beat the woman's head on the bars with such ferocity she cracked the back of her head open like an egg. With a sudden crunching sound, all the woman's movement stopped and her body slumped to the floor. Bubbles then turned toward Marco and although she had no clue, the look in her eyes caused a tremor of fear to run through him.

"Let me out this fucking cage," she demanded, as she huffed and puffed.

Marco once again spoke to the boy, who in turn went into the cage, lumped the dead woman's body over his shoulder and disappeared up the stairs.

"Will I have to use this..." Marco questioned, as he raised his shirt, allowing them a full view of his pistol on his side.

"No...Just open the damn cage Marco"

Bubbles said calmly as she impatiently waited at the cage ' s entrance.

Marco lowered his shirt. If the women had not been so high on the adrenaline rush and excitement of the kill, they would have noticed how nervous Marco had become in the last few minutes.

"I'll give you two some time to get cleaned up and I'll be back with your payment..."

He moved so fast it was as if he'd vanished into then air. The only sound marking his departure being the door slamming at the top of those dark ass stairs.

Bubbles and Buttons were visibly shaken by the ordeal as they stared silently at each other.

"Did that really happen," Bubbles

asked quietly. The dark truth dawning on her hyped up mind.

"Yea...it really happened. We just killed two people..." Realization was hitting home and hard with both of them.

Throughout their long friendship Bubbles had always known Buttons to follow her lead with no questions and had expected her statement to end at 'people' but to her surprise, there was more.

"Hold on Bubbles, let me speak", Buttons said as she placed her hands on Bubbles' shoulder.

"Ever since we met five years ago I've been rolling with you doing whatever, wherever, whenever with no questions asked. I decided to follow you here and I'm ready to get what I asked for and we're here until we are able to do something about it so rather than thinking about what we doing, I want to think about how much we're making."

"You're right Buttons.... this is some real sick shit, but we're here because we chose to be here and we may not ever be able to go back home. The best thing for us to do is make this fucking money. "

The women then took showers and minutes later Marco and the boy came down to the basement carrying a tray with meats, fruits and wine. Marco had two large wads of cash in his hands similar to the ones he had at the strip club.

"Did I forget to tell you with every kill you get an extra five thousand dollars," Marco said as he threw the wad of cash on their bed.

Their eyes bulged at the large payout

placed in front of them. They each grabbed a wad and joyfully flipped through the bills.

"A thousand dollars a day and five thousand every time we win sounds real good but something in me don't like it that I'm killing innocent people.. and won't the police look into these missing persons?" Bubbles asked.

Marco just laughed.

"Innocent people... there are no innocent people in this business. Most of your opponents are convicted criminals or drug addicts. No one will miss them and the police won't look for them because they are supplied to me by our corrections system for a small fee."

"Ok, if you say so Marco but let me make this clear, there is one thing we will not do and that is fight each other," Bubbles said.

Marco simply smiled. If only these two knew just how terrified he really was and who had the "real" power in this situation, he'd be locked in the basement; not the other way round.

"You are my gladiators...I never planned on pitting you two against each other..."

While they consumed the food and wine, Bubbles was just full of all types of questions.

"So when can we go out and enjoy some of this money and get a tour of this new country of ours?"

Marco, of course, had an answer for everything. Ah, such well laid plans of mice and...

"For now you will stay here only until your two weeks of training are up.. I want to make sure you are skilled enough to survive until your lady fight. Don't think of it as having money you can't spend.. think of it as money in the bank. Now that you have proven you are tough enough to be here, my little helper will bring down some equipment you two can work out with if you please."

Now that you mentioned it your little helper is around so much we would just like to know his name" Buttons said.

Marco walked towards the stairs and just before he took one step up...

"You can call him little Joe and he will be down shortly with workout equipment and then your dinner..." In a flash, he was up the stairs and closing the door behind him.

****

Not long after Marco disappeared, Lil Joe reappeared with a couple sets of dumbbells and fresh towels and linen for the beds.

"Are those for us lil Joe," Bubbles asked him as he went to place the dumbbells in the corner by the cage.

Lil Joe turned suddenly, surprised to hear his name called. He quickly headed for the stairs. In Joe's mind, these women were not to be played with.

"I just wanted to say thank you," Bubbles said with a smile.

"You're welcome" the boy answered in perfect English as he hurried up the stairs.

"He speaks English as good as we do. You think he's here because he wants to be or because he has to be," Buttons asked Bubbles.

Bubbles was already working a plan in her mind concerning Lil Joe. *He may turn out to be just the "little helper" we need* she thought to herself.

"I'm not sure, but, if we run into trouble he may be of use to us. Every now and then we have to talk to him when we get a chance, just to get him to warm up to us."

Just as the women talked Lil Joe came back down the stairs with more workout equipment. No time like the present!

"You must be a strong man to be able to see the things you see without breaking down or losing your mind," Bubbles said to him in an effort to get his attention, but Lil Joe pretty much ignored her statement and started back up the stairs.

"I guess he don't want to talk to us," Bubbles said.

"You must have forgot what you taught me on communicating with men," Buttons replied with a slick smile and seduction on her mind.

"And what the hell is that supposed to mean?"

"I'll show you bitch, if he comes down those steps again," Buttons said with a twinkle in her eyes.

Fortunately for them, Lil Joe once again came down the stairs with more exercise equipment. He set up the remainder of the equipment and as he started to head back up the stairs, Buttons called out to him..

"Hey Joe look at this!"

Joe turned around and his feet became glued to the spot while his eyes bulged glued to Buttons. She had taken off her top and was giving Joe a full on view of her beautiful double D's. At this point, his eyes weren't the only thing bulging!

"You learned well.." Bubbles whispered, with a smirk on her face, "..men's heads are on their necks but their brains are between their legs."

Buttons approached Joe slowly, while she slightly jiggled and bounced her enormous tits mesmerizing him as if he had fallen under Dracula ' s hypnotizing stare.

"If you think they look fun, imagine how good they feel," Bubbles said seductively, locking her eyes to his.

Joe, Bubbles and Buttons

While they walked towards Joe, Bubbles tantalized him by licking and sucking on Buttons' dark nipples causing them to harden along with Lil Joe. He began massaging his bulge of sexual excitement as he watched their exhibition with growing anticipation .

"Instead of touching that how about touching these," Buttons said as she pushed her large bosom in lil Joe's face. He reached out, grabbed hold of one, hungrily sucking on it like a baby being breast fed.

While Joe suckled Buttons' breast, his hands began to travel her body, exploring the wet, warmth between her thighs. Meanwhile, Bubbles was busy massaging the expanding bulge in his pants.

"You see Lil Joe, we can all be very

good friends if you would like us to be," Bubbles said in a sensual tone.

Just as she was about to unzip Joe's pants and really get busy, they were interrupted by Marco calling out in Russian. Like a dog hearing his master, Lil Joe's body stiffened. He quickly zipped up his pants and flew up the stairs.

"Damn we almost had him," Buttons said with a grin on her face.

"No, we got him and I promise you he'll be back for more" Bubbles replied.

****

Later that night as Bubbles and Buttons slept, the door at the top of the stairs slowly opened. Footsteps could be heard hitting each step as they were led by a bright light. The light went down into the basement, the gleam breaking Button's sleep as it lit on her face. Buttons then softly shook Bubbles awake as they both shielded their eyes from the bright light.

"What is it now Marco," Bubbles said in a sleepy and aggravated tone.

"It's not him... it's me," a familiar voice said from behind the bright light.

The light then lowered from their faces and in its glow they saw a buck naked Lil Joe standing before them.

"I told you he would be back," Bubbles laughed.

Bubbles and Buttons climbed out of bed, laying Lil Joe in their place on his back.

"Have you ever been with a woman," Bubbles whispered to him.

"No. .. That was my first time ever touching any part of a woman other than a couple of hugs his from my mom," Joe nervously answered.

Bubbles quickly unzipped Joe's pants, eager to discover the source behind the bulge. She pulled down his boxers and out jumped a long, fat, swollen arrow pointed directly at her.

"Oohh...I like that," Buttons whispered. She grabbed his dick and slowly started to stroke it. "Damn you hung like a horse! You look nine inches strong. How old are you? Young girls your age taking all this dick?" She couldn't wait to fill it slide between both sets of her now moistened lips.

"I'm nineteen and the girls my age do have a little trouble with me" Joe laughed.

Joe, Bubbles and Buttons

"Damn you packing! From now on I'm a just call you Joe because there ain't nothing lil about you. Let me taste that dick first," Bubbles said.

"We're not just gonna give you your first experience with two women but we're going to show you how to satisfy a woman also...First thing is knowing how to eat some pussy," Buttons said, as she climbed on top of Joe and pushed her warm pussy into his face. "This big ass of mine ain't to much for you huh honey?" Buttons asked.

"While you take care of her I'm going to take care of you," Bubbles said as she tongued the shaft of Joe's dick.

"Ahhhh....What's that feeling....I love it" Joe said, as his legs trembled from Bubbles' tongue sliding up and down his stiff dick.

"That's called sexual stimulation," Buttons answered, "now it's time for you to do the same for me." She wiggled her ass to get her wet box a bit closer to his lips.

"So what am I suppose to do with this thing" Joe asked innocently, liking and not liking the smell as it connected with his nose, yet feeling an excitement like he'd never felt before. The urge to lick the thing was getting stronger with each passing moment.

"Less talking and more tasting is a good start" Buttons said as she spread the lips of her pussy open to reveal a hardened and glistening clit.

"Now stick your tongue in there and pretend that you are eating ice cream out of a sugar cone," Buttons said.

Joe, Bubbles and Buttons

"Ice cream...I don't see any ice cream," Joe responded, wrinkling his nose and looking deeper inside her opened pussy.

Buttons just laughed "if you do it right you are going to definitely see some ice cream."

Joe then slowly inserted his tongue between Buttons' pussy lips and she giggled as his tongue tickled her swollen clitoris. Once his tongue made contact with her clit, he instinctively began to suck on it and play with it, causing Buttons to spasm and squirm about on his face. *He's not gonna need much teaching* she contemplated as she began to grind her behind on the tip of Joe's now intruding tongue.

While Joe was tongue deep in Buttons' pussy, Bubbles had taken his fully erect dick down her throat. It seemed as if the harder Joe had his dick sucked, the more intensely he munched into Buttons' pussy.

Joe's body began to stiffen, his legs trembling as his load built up ready to release into Bubbles' throat. Almost simultaneously Buttons' back arched and she pushed his face deeper into her drooling pussy as she neared climax.

"Ahhh... " Buttons moaned in pleasure as a flood of cream raced down Joe's chin. As he lapped up Buttons' milk, he too exploded filling Bubbles' throat with his release and she eagerly swallowed it down in gulps with ease.

"For a Lil man you pack a lot of cum," Bubbles said as she was forced to pull away and wiped away the over flow.

"It's my turn now sis," Bubbles said to

Joe, Bubbles and Buttons

Buttons signaling her eagerness to be pleased. What she really wanted was to feel all nine of those inches pounding her pussy walls. Her lady gushed and she squirmed just from the thought.

Just as Bubbles and Buttons began to trade places, Joe's eyes bucked and he quickly jumped out of the bed as if he had seen a ghost.

"What's wrong, "Buttons asked.

Joe then pointed to a red light blinking on the ceiling in the corner of the room, "I forgot about the cameras..."

"Cameras?" Bubbles spoke to his back as Joe quickly made his way up the stairs and disappeared into the house.

"You think that twisted ass Marco saw what was going on?" Buttons asked.

"I don't know but I sure hope we didn't

get our little friend into trouble" Bubbles responded.

Bubbles and Buttons could not really get much sleep that night; they worried that Marco had indeed witnessed their sexual adventure with Joe. So they sat up listening for any signs of Joe being chastised for his moment of weakness but surprisingly there was nothing but silence and they eventually fell asleep.

The next morning, they were awakened by the sound of dishes clanking and the aroma of breakfast being served.

Joe set up breakfast for them and started cleaning out the cage without looking in their direction once. After he finished, he headed back for the stairs without a word or glance at the ladies.

"Hey Joe, how you doing this morning?" Buttons asked him with an uneasy smile on her face.

Joe stopped in his tracks, turning around to speak, "the training is going to start early today so it's best you two eat and get ready soon."

Joe's words showed signs of everything being normal but his body language, demeanor and his tone gave them reason to think otherwise. Shortly after he disappeared behind the infamous door, Marco came down to them.

"Good morning.. today our training will begin a little early because I have a special guest joining us so hurry your breakfast and get prepared," Marco said as he sipped his coffee and went up the stairs. If he knew anything of last night's activities, he wasn't letting on.

"Do you think he knows," Buttons asked Bubbles as she dressed.

"I don't know...I can't tell so just act normal" Bubbles whispered.

A few minutes later, Marco, Lil Joe and some grotesquely obese and hairy guy in a uniform who wreaked of alcohol and cheap cigarettes came bounding down the stairs. The ladies immediately disliked this new fellow added to the mix and knew some extra level of bullshit was about to be incorporated.

"Bubbles, Buttons... This is my good friend Andre. He's the warden of the correctional facility that supplies our training and entertainment. Whenever I have promising gladiators, he's always welcome to test their abilities before my regular clients," Marco said as he walked over to the guy and shook his hand.

Strangely, this Andre had a long chain in his left hand that extended all the way up the stairs. When he tugged at the chain, it slowly started to come down the stairs followed by two beastly women attached to the other end.

`"Get yourselves ready quickly.. my friend is on a time schedule," Marco barked.

Bubbles walked over to Marco with hands on hips and anger dripping from her like acid..

"What the fuck are those Marco?! We agreed to fight only women and they ain't women. We will..."

Marco interrupted her with a quiet yet vicious response.

"You are not here to decide who you are fighting..you are here only to fight. I can put a rabid dog in there and you will fight or die. I pay you and provide everything you need to win, the rest is up to you. Now stop embarrassing me in front of my guest. Start fighting or I'll have both your asses skinned alive!"

Bubbles then walked over to Buttons, " I'll go first this time."

"Are you sure," Buttons asked.

"Yea...I'm sure. You did the dirty deed first last time, remember?"

Andre had the women he brought in chained to the back wall shackled from head to feet. Marco said something to Lil Joe so he released one of the women from her shackles and led her into the cage. Compared to the women they fought before, these were nightmares.They looked drugged out of their minds like the first two women but these two were covered in scars and bruises like they had been fighting their entire lives and they resembled more neanderthal women than modern day women.

Bubbles slowly entered the cage with her eyes fixed on her opponent until her back was firmly against the corner of the cage. Buttons stood outside the cage gripping her fingers firmly through the bars as Marco approached her opponent with that leather case of his.

For just a second, Bubbles turned her head and glanced at Lil Joe standing outside of the cage door waiting to remove the corpse of the loser. He gave Bubbles a slight head nod and she responded with a smile.

"FIGHT!"

In the same instant, Bubbles turned around, grit her teeth and rushed her opponent with everything she had. Her opponent had the same thing in mind; she had started charging at the word fight also and they both violently clashed in the middle of the cage like two wild cats.

Buttons stood by watching nervously as Bubbles and the woman slam each other against the cage. Marco and Andre shared drinks and laughed in enjoyment at this brutal entertainment.

Bubbles and the woman screamed and yelled as they slammed each other against the cage. Bubbles pushed her hands into the woman's face and drove her into the side of the cage but unfortunately for her the woman caught the top of her left pinky finger in her teeth and crunched down.

"AHHH YOU BITCH!" Bubbles yelled as she felt tendons, muscles and bones ripping in her hand. Buttons picked up her right leg, wedged it between herself and the woman, forcefully pushing her to the ground.

The woman slowly rose to her feet all the while chewing on something hard and bloody, staring at Bubbles with blood shot eyes through a veil of ragged hair that draped her face.

The shock was wearing off because Bubbles suddenly felt sharp and intense pain coming from her left hand. She slowly lifted her hand to see blood squirting from a bloody stump where the tip of her finger used to be. She then looked at the woman chewing, realizing the woman was chewing on her fingertip just as she swallowed.

The woman began yelling again as she and Bubbles raced towards each other but this time instead of a head on collision Bubbles dropped kicked the woman smashing her face and sending blood and teeth flying all over the cage.

Bubbles hurried towards the woman, grabbed her head and just started pounding the living hell out of her. The intensity at which she slammed her head into the cage floor showed Bubbles was more than capable of crossing the line in taking a human life; a fact Marco was more than proud of . When Bubbles' opponent's head cracked open and spilled her brains, Marco yelled out in excitement as he collected money from Andre.

Bubbles then slowly rose to her feet and exited the cage as Lil Joe went in to remove the splattered corpse of the woman. Once outside, she received a tight embrace from Buttons " you alright? "

`"Yea... I'm fine," Bubbles responded in a slow, calm tone.

Buttons started to make her way into the cage but was stopped by Marco.

"I am eager to see the fight as much as you are eager *to* fight but I want to keep it a fair fight. Wait until Joe cleans the rest of your friend's opponent out of the cage."

While Lil Joe mopped up the remains, Andre got up from his seat and walked over to Buttons, eyeing her from head to toe "you are thick like Clydesdale...I like that. " He grabbed a handful of her ass and squeezed but before he could release his grip, Buttons punched lightning out of his ass and sent him flying across the floor.

Marco grabbed his gun from his waist and rushed towards Buttons harshly yelling in Russian. Bubbles tried to get in front of Marco but he knocked her to the side with the butt of his pistol. He stood in front of Buttons, put his gun up to her head and...

"NO! STOP!"

While lying on his back, Andre lifted his head to the side of his large stomach and yelled out with a dark smile on his face...

"She's tough...I like that."

Marco lowered his pistol...

"He is a well paying customer. He pay me and I pay you for his pleasure and entertainment; that is how my business works. Until our businesses is done, you hurt my business and I hurt you, are we clear? "

He eyed both Bubbles and Buttons.

"Crystal..." they both replied in unison.

Andre rolled onto his side, hoisted himself to his feet and went over to Marco.

"The party is just beginning..I don't mind a little foreplay," he said with his dark smile.

Marco said something to Andre in Russian and they both laughed hard as they walked back over to the cage. Lil Joe had just finished cleaning and had already led the other woman inside. Buttons took a couple of deep breaths and entered.

Marco wanted this training session to really test Bubbles and Buttons so he gave their height, weights and fighting ability information to Andre so he could pick women in the prison that would give them an adequate challenge.

The woman sat in a dead-like stupor in the cage, covered in rags and filth. Her head, shoulders and bodies slumped over; her eyes barely open with drool hanging from her dry, cracked lips. Buttons stood a stout six foot two but by her opponent being barely able to stand, seemed a few inches taller or shorter. Who could tell?

That question was answered once Marco gave her his magic formula, turning the degenerate drug addict into a raging beast. A few scant moments after the injection, the woman rose to a towering six foot five, her eyes widened, blood shot, as she began screaming like some mad wild animal. Once Marco yelled the word 'fight', the women went into immediate attack mode as if they had been trained to do so.

The woman immediately rushed Buttons. She tried to sidestep her but the woman countered, grabbed Buttons, lifted her off her feet, throwing her to the ground hard and fast. Buttons raced to her feet, bracing herself against the cage to keep her opponent in front of her. The woman was puffing, yelling and circling Buttons, planning her next attack. The woman then rushed Buttons. Buttons braced herself against the cage and violently kicked the woman in her chest. She stumbled backward from the impact of the kick, wiped blood from her chin she spit up and began yelling at the top of her lungs.

Buttons couldn't believe the woman's reaction! With the force she'd put into that kick, she thought it would at least put her on the ground. She was also surprised the woman hardly flinched from that powerful blow to the chest!

Bubbles knew Buttons was definitely in a fight for her life with this one, so she moved closer to the cage to grabbed her hands to let her know she was there for support. Buttons felt her but kept her focus on the madwoman glaring at her, who was preparing to charge again.

This time Buttons charged also and they clashed in the middle of the cage like two unmovable objects. They grabbed each other in any place their hands could find a hold and tried to overpower each other. Buttons knew she was a strong woman but realized her opponent was stronger because, at the moment, she was the one giving up ground in the struggle.

Thinking quickly, she surmised it would take more than brute strength and ferocity to win this fight; she would have to out think this bitch.

Buttons allowed the woman to build momentum in pushing her backwards then used the woman's momentum in reverse and slung her against the cage. With her back against the cage, the woman clawed at Buttons furiously while Buttons held her up and started kneeling her in the sides and midsection. The more she did, she could feel the woman's body begin to buckle under the blows.

The woman opened her mouth, forcing her face forward as if she was intent on taking a bite out of Buttons' face but before she could get close enough to clamp down on anything, Buttons, feeling she had the strength advantage, used all her might to sling the woman to the ground.

"YEA BUTTONS GET THAT BITCH! GET THAT BITCH" Bubbles yelled as she jumped up and down with excitement.

Andre was smiling when his fighter had the advantage but watching Bubbles take her to the ground, his smile turned to a frown as he reached into his wallet for more money while Marco eyed him with a look of pride.

Once the woman hit the ground, it was

pretty much a done deal. Buttons began kicking and stomping the woman in the head and chest. The more she stomped, the less the woman fought. Every blow reduced her life span and everyone could tell.

She continued to stomp the woman until she was nothing more than a bloody pulp on the ground yet she still showed signs of life as blood leaked from her mouth with every shallow breath she took. Buttons stood over the woman, turning to Marco, "I hope this it's not the best you can do..."

Buttons then placed her foot on the woman's throat and slowly started to use her body weight as pressure until there was a loud pop; blood rushed from the woman's nose and mouth then she went completely limp.

This kill changed the lives of Bubbles and Buttons. No matter what they ever went through, those last moments permanently altered and scarred them both forever. By overcoming opponents that had an advantage over them, they had now taken their first steps to becoming skilled fighters and trained assassins.

After Buttons brutally dispatched her rival, she spit on the corpse, walking out the ring with the pride and confidence of a peacock.

****

Andre handed over to Marco the money in his hands as Marco then shouted some orders to Lil Joe in Russian; he went up the stairs and into the house. He quickly returned with a large suitcase, handing it to Marco before removing the corpse from the cage.

Bubbles and Buttons started cleaning themselves off, but when Marco heard the water running in their sink, he quickly and loudly yelled,

"NO.. STOP! "

He pointed at them while yelling orders to Lil Joe in Russian and he raced over to Bubbles and Buttons.

"What's wrong Joe? We're just trying to clean up a bit, " Bubbles said.

"You can't wash up...you're not finished yet..."

"Not finished yet?! What the fuck does that mean? We just killed two fucking..people what more can he want from us?" Buttons angrily asked.

Bubbles, the more worldly of the two, angrily asked.

`"Are you saying that fat, nasty muthafucka wants us to fuck him with all this blood and shit on us?!"

Lil Joe nodded his head "yes."

Buttons stormed over to Marco about as fed up as any woman could be, "DO WE REALLY HAVE TO FUCK THIS FAT SON OF BITCH LIKE THIS?!"

"This **fat son of a bitch,** as you so eloquently put it, is a paying customer and friend of mine, so you and your fucking friend better get real fucking horny real fucking fast! "

Marco then says something in Russian to Lil Joe and he once again disappears into the house.

"You two have a job to do and you

better do it. I will be watching... I am always watching," Marco barked as he went up the stairs to also disappear behind the door that separated them from freedom.

After the door closed behind Marco, Andre opened the suitcase Joe had brought from inside the house and look at Bubbles and Buttons with that dark smile of his. He then pulled a bull whip out and calmly stated..

"Don't worry.. since this is our first time I won't be too rough..."

"Ok let's get this over with," Bubbles said as she started taking off her blood soaked clothes.

"You alright," Buttons asked her, following suit.

"I'm fine..." there was a sigh of

acceptance in that statement "...I'm just ready to get this over, get our money and get this fucking guy out of here... Aren't you?"

"No matter how much we argue, we end up doing exactly what that son-of-a-bitch Marco tells us anyway, so why waste time. He might want us to do some weird and crazy shit but as long as he don't permanently fuck up nothing on our body there's only so much he can do to us. He's not gonna kill us...that's for damn sure. We can bring in too much for that... "

"Of course I'm not going to kill you. I just like a little blood with my steak..."

Andre laughed as he walked towards the two with the whip in hand.

"But it is strange how Marco is training two girls this time.. he usually only trains one at a time."

"You're right Bubbles, let's get this shit over with real quick..." Buttons said, as she finished undressing.

"So what do you plan on doing with that whip?" Bubbles asked Andre.

Andre stretched the whip out in his hands, "I am the warden of all prisons in Russia. Ten years ago there was a riot in my prison and I was captured. The prisoners castrated me."

Andre took off his gun belt and his pants, revealing a bare patch of skin where his dick and balls should have been. Both their faces dropped in shock at such an unthinkable sight. A man without a dick...UNTHINKABLE!!!

"Even though I have no more sex parts, I am still a man and still have cravings, so

I have learned to satisfy them by substituting pleasure for pain. This whip is for me, when I get sexually stimulated and need to experience sexual release, I provide myself with pain and my needs are met..."

Andre then took off his shirt and exposed his entire upper body was covered in whelp marks from the whip.

"Man that's crazy but if it's what you are paying for then that's what we're going to give you," Bubbles said.

Andre walked over to Buttons, handing her the whip..

"You are a thick, strong woman.. I want you to start and finish while she fills in between." He walked over to the bed, sat down, pulled out a pack of cigarettes and lit one.

Buttons walked over to him, grabbed the cigarette out his mouth, took a slow pull off of it, blew smoke in his face then...

WHAP !

Buttons then slapped Andre so hard he rolled back onto the bed.

"What the fuck you did that for," Bubbles asked her.

"I don't know it just felt right," Buttons replied calmly. She'd slapped him so hard, it left a red hand print on the side of his face.

Andre raised up on the bed with a frown of pain on his face and started rubbing the slap indentation with his dark, sadistic smile,

"You give such wonderful pain you big bitch... I want more!"

Bubbles and Buttons burst out in

laughter "Don't worry you fat muthafucka, we have more where that came from" Bubbles said, as she slapped him on the opposite cheek.

Andre laughed as he lit another cigarette and laid back on the bed.

"Give me more. .."

"I got you baby," Buttons said as she grabbed the whip from Bubbles and walked to the bed. Pulled a chair in front of the bed, she slowly finished stripping off her clothes as Andre watched with saucer sized eyes.

While sitting in the chair, she spread her legs and started to massage her clit with the hand grip of the whip; with her other hand, she continued to puff on the cigarette. Bubbles walked up behind Buttons to massage her plump breast.

"I wanna play too," she whined seductively.

As Bubbles and Buttons performed for Andre, his anticipation of pleasure had him rubbing his hairy chest and squirming on the bed "yes...yes I like that."

After a few more pulls off the cigarette, Buttons got up, walked over to Andre and ground the cigarette out on the void between his legs where his dick once rested.

"Ohhh yes..." Andre uttered in painful pleasure.

"You can't have all the fun. Even though your dick is gone, you can still use your tongue can't you?" Buttons asked a smoking Andre.

"Oh yes... I do still love eating some pussy," Andre eagerly replied.

"Girl go sit on his fucking face and feed that muthafucka some of that good pussy of yours" Buttons winked at Bubbles.

Bubbles walked over to the bed, "lay your fat ass down so I can feed you this pussy."

"I want your friend to start pleasuring me so you come here and let me hold you to my face," Andre said. Bubbles walked to the bed.

"Now climb into my arms," Andre told her. Bubbles climbed into Andre's arms and he positioned her pussy right in front of his mouth.

Andre sat up in the bed on his knees with Bubbles in his arms and braced her back against the wall as he dug his face deep inside her moist pussy.

"Hold on girl here comes the pain," Buttons yelled as she rolled the whip in her hands ready to unleash it on Andre. Bubbles tried to respond but she had a lump in her throat as Andre hungrily ate her dripping pussy. Andre had Bubbles ' s eyes rolling partially back in her head from his tongue activity.

Buttons then raised her arm high above her head, brought it down and forward to lash Andre's back.

WHACK!

As the whip struck Andre's back, blood and flesh ripped, causing an ugly gash yet surprisingly all Andre did was flinch slightly without missing a beat as his tongue stayed buried deep inside Bubbles. As the whip hit Andre's back, his slight flinch caused him to jab his tongue deeper into pussy-land which made her release a slight yelp. The sight of the whip lashing at his back and particles of flesh and blood exploding from his body, made Buttons tremble, stiffening up from the shock.

She swallowed hard, took a deep breath, rolled the whip in her hands and released it upon Andre once again with the same result as before. He flinched slightly, again jabbing Bubbles' clit with his tongue and causing her to yelp out in pleasure.

After getting those first few hits and the sight of tearing flesh out of her system, Buttons let loose on Andre for a solid ten minutes, only stopping because her arms became tired of swinging the whip. Besides the multiple scars on Andre's back, it was evident his body was used to the punishment; the only real damage the whip doing was to open superficial wounds. Andre's flesh had toughen from massive punishment.

"My arms are killing me.. I can't go anymore," Buttons said, half out of breath.

Andre once again pulled his cream covered face from Bubbles' soaked opening..

"That felt amazing! The power you possess! Now, you two trade places and once she gets tired, you finish it off."

Bubbles climbed out of Andre's arms and walked over to where Buttons stood still holding the whip.

"Did that really feel as good as it looked," Buttons asked Bubbles with a big smile as she handed her the whip.

"That muthafucka ate my fucking

brains out through my ass...Girl yessss," Bubbles replied, with her pussy still dripping spit and cum.

Buttons then walked over to Andre on the bed with her hands gripping her ample bottom.

"Now I'm a bit thicker than she is so you think you can handle all this ass and pussy," Buttons asked him while she palmed and kneaded her ass.

"All that and more," Andre replied arrogantly.

She then climbed into Andre's hairy arms as he dove head first into her pussy, going to work. Bubbles stood behind him with the whip in her hands, building herself up to even throw the first lash. She rolled the bloody whip in her hands, swung it out at Andre and struck his back.

SMACK! It stuck home!

Buttons jerked and yelped as Andre's tongue drove deeper into her pussy from the sensation of the whip striking his flesh...

****

Bubbles thrashed Andre until her arms tired also and once she was finished, Buttons took control of beating the pleasure out of him. After about ten more minutes of the brutal back lashings, Buttons' was worn out and their service to Andre had concluded.

After the job was complete, they all started putting their clothes back on, and Andre voiced his pleasure in their performance of services rendered.

"You two are both tough and sexy

women, that will also help you to be very successful in this business. It is a hard business but then, you two are very hard women..."

"Yea if we can survive," Buttons responded with a bit of a worried look. The last two had been vicious...what could they expect next?

Andre laughed, "I have faith you two will be the first to survive all fights and leave here very wealthy."

"Leave here very wealthy...really? We are killing people every day. What assurances do we have that you and your friend upstairs will let us out of here alive. We've been just doing what we're being told but how do we know you won't kill us or turn us in to the police," Bubbles asked.

Andre laughed. This time the laugh

was something akin to evil.

"I am the Head of Federal police and prisons in Russia remember? So no crime gets punished without my approval and you two are serving more pleasure than pain...In my book, what you are doing is no crime and my book is the only one that matters..."

As they talked, the door to the house opened with Marco leaping down the steps and Lil Joe trailing behind him.

"Did you enjoy yourself my friend," Marco asked Andre as they shook hands.

"I greatly enjoyed it my friend. That was the best experience I ever had! These two are indeed something special and will make a lot of money and a lot of people happy in more ways than one."

Andre then grabbed and kissed Bubbles and Buttons hands like a true gentleman which surprised the hell out of both of them, considering.

"It was a pleasure! I hope we get another opportunity to play together and soon."

Andre then disappeared up the stairs and into the house.

Marco had come down with two large envelopes in hand and gave one to each. He was wearing that twisted smile of his like some sick, proud Poppa. He was beaming!

"Well done ladies! You're both becoming great warriors and pleasure toys."

Bubbles flipped her fingers through

the stack of bills in the envelope, counting as she went.

"So I guess we're gonna have to fuck you next huh?"

"I only test your skills before I hire you.. once you start working for me, I keep business as business. After I ensure you have the necessary skills for my clients, I train you to be gladiators and from now on if you need more sexual stimulation or training, Andre is always available. I prefer you not practice with Lil Joe," Marco replied.

"So you saw huh? I hope we didn't get him into any trouble," Buttons said.

"Like I said before, I am always watching and Joe is not in any trouble. He is a young man and has urges just as we all do.. I just prefer he keep business separate and you two do the same or there will be consequences," With that said, Marco disappeared upstairs.

The entire time Bubbles and Buttons were in Russia, they were apprehensive of their futures. Regardless of how much money they made or how much they pleased Marco, they always remembered Marco was in complete control and would kill them if it at all benefited him. Instead of just waiting to find out what would happen if and when they fulfilled their agreement with Marco, they agreed to decide their own fate.

Later on that night Bubbles whispered

to Buttons as they laid in bed..

"Buttons? Buttons, don't get up..we can just whisper back and forth just like this ok?"

"Ok," Buttons replied.

"I'm starting to have seconds thoughts about being here. It's starting to smell like bullshit to me... this is just a bunch of dog ass men using women for their own pleasure and entertainment and that means we can beat them because regardless of how smart they seem, they still do most of their thinking with the head in between their legs and that means they're weak. My only concern is for Lil Joe, I think they kidnapped him," Bubbles said in an angry whisper.

"I'm starting to feel the same way about everything, but you do know in order to get away from them before our last fight...we have to kill them," Buttons replied matter-of-factly.

"I know... we just have to wait until the right moment before we make our move."

Before going to sleep that night, they talked about possible options to get them out of their current situation in one piece, free and alive.

3

The Good Life

Finally Buttons and Bubbles had completed their training in that wretched basement! After fourteen long days of fighting for their lives, they earned the right to live inside the house. They would still have to fight for their lives for another ten weeks but at least they would be able to enjoy the comforts of 'home'.

After their final hard fought victory in the basement, Marco had Joe escort them to a bathroom inside the house to get cleaned up. Even though this was just the beginning of another gauntlet for them, they did have some sense of accomplishment for making it out of that hellish place alive.

"When you are finished cleaning up, Joe will bring you to meet me in the social room," Marco said to them as they disappeared up the stairs with Joe for the first time.

When they'd first arrived, they'd had a glimpse of the house but now as Joe led them to the bathroom they really saw it's splendor. The entire house was lined, floored and walled with marble and gold along with elegant statues and paintings beautifying every available space. There was classical music gently resonating through the walls and a soft scent of cinnamon hung in the air.

Joe led them up three flights of spiraling marble and gold staircase, down a long statue lined hallway to a huge room that resembled those of only royalty. It was truly a sight to behold.

"This is fucking amazing," Bubbles said with glimmers in her eyes.

"Yeah...it's nice," Joe responded, "this will be your room. It's more than enough for two people and there are new clothes in the closet. I'll be back in thirty minutes to take you to meet Marco..." Having said that, he was gone in a flash.

Buttons jumped on the bed as Bubbles toured the room and is contents. The room was about the size of three regular rooms with a huge walk-in closet. Inside were different sets of clothes marked with each woman's name.

"This is what I'm talking about! This is how we deserve to live," Buttons said.

"This and more..." Bubbles responded, as

she went into the bathroom.

Thirty minutes later Lil Joe returned; Bubbles and Buttons were dressed in sexy evening attire awaiting his arrival.

"These clothes fit us like we bought them for ourselves...that's creepy in some type of way. How is this possible," Bubbles asked Joe.

"We have computer systems that tell us your height and weight through the cameras. As you can see, Marco doesn't mind spending money for the best quality" Joe responded.

They followed Joe back down the marble and gold spiral staircase to the second floor and down another long elaborate hallway to a large room filled with more elaborate statues and paintings.

In the center of the room was a large

glass table with food and wine with Marco sitting at the head. Marco raised his glass in a toast..

"Welcome ladies! You have now made it to the big time. Please ladies... come sit and enjoy."

As Bubbles, Buttons and Joe took their seats at the table, Marco poured wine in everyone's glass including Joe.

"You letting him drink at his age?" Buttons asked Marco.

"You're asking me about letting him drink when you and your friend were ready to fucked his brains in the other day," Marco replied with a nasty smirk.

"That's different...pussy and some head ain't going to ruin his life," Buttons jokingly replied.

Marco smiled, "now that you two have

made it to the big leagues, you will now stay in the house and if you like Joe will take you into town to shop or whatever you wish. The only limitation you have is don't talk to anyone about anything or you might cause them to lose their life and you yours. Oh... no cell phones or any type of communication devices. You all can leave now but your first performance is tomorrow night so I suggest you give yourselves enough time to rest. "

"Joe can drive too?!," Buttons asked, shocked and adding this info to the plan forming in her head.

"He may *seem* limited but he is a very privileged young man and enjoys many freedoms," Marco replied.

Bubbles jumped up, pointing at Joe, "come on kid get your keys and let's get the hell out of here!" Buttons and Joe jumped out their seats, making a B-line for the door. They made it outside just as Lil Joe hit a button on the key ring to jump start a black Rolls Royce Phantom parked in the long, circular driveway. They hopped in and off they went, leaving dust in their wake.

"So where we headed," Buttons asked Joe.

"We are headed for downtown Moscow," Joe answered.

"So that's where we are... Moscow huh? Marco told us we were in Russia but not in Moscow. We know why we are here... So, what's your story," Bubbles asked Lil Joe, studying his face for any signs of discomfort.

"Every since I can remember Marco

has been my guardian...that's about all I can tell you."

"Are you happy there with all the killing and shit that goes on," Buttons asked pointedly.

"At first it was uncomfortable for me but now I'm used to it," Joe replied with complete honesty.

As Joe finished his statement, he pulled into a enormous parking lot.

"This is the largest mall in Russia... would you like to stop here first?" He parked the Rolls close to the entrance.

"Hell yeah," Buttons responded gleefully, hopping out the car...

****

Bubbles, Buttons and Joe hit almost every part of downtown Moscow, spending great gobs of money before heading back to the house that night.

When they arrived back at the house, they found Marco sitting at a desk in the entryway as if he had been waiting for them to return.

"I hope we weren't out too late huh dad," Bubbles said jokingly to Marco.

At first Marco had a look of confusion on his face trying to process what Bubbles said but once he realized what she meant he broke out in laughter.

Eager to put her bags down, Bubbles instinctively headed towards the door leading to the basement. Realizing her mistake, she froze as she grabbed the doorknob and slowly turned around to see if anyone caught her error. Buttons, Marco and Joe all stood silently staring at her.

"If you prefer that room over your new

one, you are more than welcome to it," Marco told her with a wink.

"Fuck that," Bubbles said as she quickly headed for the spiral staircase.

"Make sure you two get some rest, you have a long day tomorrow," Marco said as he disappeared down the hallway.

"A long day...we don't fight until tomorrow night. What the hell did he mean by that..." Bubbles directed her question at Joe.

Joe hunched his shoulders to signal 'I don't know' just as Marco yelled to him in Russian from the dark hallway. Joe hurried down the hallway toward the sound of Marco's voice.

****

That night they talked as they laid in the massive king sized bed...

"Maybe this won't be so bad," Bubbles said.

"Today was a good day but what about tomorrow or the next day or the next. We had good days at Bandits too but we had more bad ones and this is just the same old shit except we make more money and take bigger risks," Buttons angrily whispered.

"Yea you're right of course," Bubbles agreed.

Buttons continued, "We are just following the orders of all these dumb ass men and allowing them to make a lot of money off of us and pay us pennies. Yeah, were making more money than we ever have but think about how much Marco is making. Don't you think we deserve that and then some?! We are the ones putting our asses and lives on the line every fucking day! "

"We *do* deserve it," Bubbles replied, feeling a little of the heat coming from Buttons' angry words.

****

The next morning instead of waking up in a dark dungeon, Bubbles and Buttons woke to a serenade of Russian opera music, the soft scent of cinnamon and breakfast in bed. While they ate their breakfast, Marco walked into the room sounding rather chipper...

"Good morning ladies. I trust you slept well."

"It was wonderful," Buttons said as she ate some toast.

"What's so busy about today? I figured we were just gonna take it easy until the fight tonight," Bubbles asked.

Marco looked at her with a frown, "Winners don't take it easy...they work constantly to keep their skills fresh. For the next ten weeks this will be your schedule. After breakfast you will train for two hours.. after lunch you will attend an opera and then prepare for your performance. "

"First of all why an opera and why do you keep saying 'our performance' like we doing a concert or something," Bubbles asked, always so full of questions.

Marco's answer was as smooth as a baby's hinny and just as eloquent.

"Violence in itself is an art and when you carry out acts of violence you are creating a work in progress which is the finished product, preferably death. You will go to the opera to learn peace and keep you balance. We work in a violent business but as human beings we need to know peace and opera is the ultimate peace..."These words were rare and a bit out of place coming from a man in Marco's line of work yet they made absolute sense.

After a long day of training and opera, Marco allowed them three hours to rest or whatever before their 'performance.'

―――――――――――

Later that night, just before fight time, Marco entered their room with two all leather bras and shorts.

"From now on you will wear these to your performances. "

`"All leather... Well I guess it beats a ragged shirt and dingy shorts," Buttons said with a smile.

"Have you two ever played baseball," Marco asked.

"Baseball...no why you ask," Bubbles responded suspiciously.

"The theme for tonight's performance is aluminum baseball bats. If either of you played baseball it would probably give you an advantage..." It was stated in such a nonchalant type of way, it was almost missed... Almost.

"What the hell you mean aluminum baseball bats?! Are we fighting with those tonight?" Buttons asked with slight concern.

"The night before every performance, myself and a few select clients hold a drawing for the theme of each performance."

"And the fun begins..." Bubbles said sarcastically.

"At our expense..." Buttons whispered testily.

Everyone, including Joe, met in the hallway leading to the door.

"Does he really have to see this?" Buttons asked.

Marco gave Buttons a hard stare but before he could respond, Joe did...

"Don't worry about me.. you're the ones fighting for your lives tonight."

Satisfied by Joe's response, Marco led everyone to a waiting limousine outside.

****

After a frigid and snow covered ride, the limousine pulled up to a large gated structure with huge marble lion statues on each side of the gate. The lions looked as if they were standing guard.

The gates opened, allowing the limousine entrance; it came to a halt in front of two large doors, seemingly the entrance to the structure. The doors of the structure opened and armed men in snow suits came out to escorted them in. Once inside the building, they were led deep into the bowels of the place until they reached a room with a cage in the center.

"You two go with those guys," Marco ordered Bubbles and Buttons.

An elevator opened up in the hallway and some of the men escorted Marco and Lil Joe inside it while the rest of the men escorted Bubbles and Buttons to the cage.

While walking to the center of the

room and possible death, Buttons looked up at her surroundings, spotting a glass encased room above them with a group of wealthy looking people including Marco and Joe standing in it. The men then led Bubbles and Buttons inside the cage and left. Buttons moved close to Bubbles and started pointing with her eyes.

"Look... they're all up there in that box looking down on us. "

Bubbles peered up at them,"how much money do you think those filthy rich muthafucka are paying Marco for this shit?!"

"I don't know but if he's able to pay us what he's paying then it has to be a helluva lot," Buttons replied.

They both laughed in a joking moment to help ease the tension but it was cut short by the appearance of more armed men escorting their opponents. Two long legged, long armed women, frizzy haired and both tattooed from head to toe. They were dressed in dirty gray overalls while the chains on their feet drug across the ground as they did a sort of slow drag marched to the cage.

One of the armed men carried a large black bag on his shoulder. Once the other women were in the cage, the man put the bag down, opening it to reveal two aluminum bats.

"You two come here and take one," he told Bubbles and Buttons. He then pulled out two more bats and literally put them in the other women's hands, closing their fingers around the grips.

"Get in the opposite corner and stay

there until you hear me announce the word fight," Marco voiced over a loudspeaker.

Bubbles and Buttons gripped their bats tightly as they raised them in readiness for combat. One of the armed men then removed the shackles and pulled out the ever present syringe filled with the clear substance. The man then injected the two women as they all quickly left the cage, locking it behind them.

Bubbles, Buttons and everyone else watched and waited for the serum to take effect, while Marco watched his watch in anticipation.

"Do you remember how long it took for that shit to work," Buttons asked Bubbles.

"I don't remember exactly but I know the shit works fast." The adrenaline had begun to pump so the ladies didn't have time to feel nerves or anything else. It was fight time!

Just as she spoke those words the women began twitching and that was Marco's cue...

"Fight!" he yelled over the speakers.

Bubbles and Buttons froze for just a second afterwards because the women were just twitching and not moving towards them. In their hesitation, their opponents woke suddenly in a rage.Within a blink of an eye, the women went from twitching husks to raging mad beasts.

As they rushed Bubbles and Buttons, they swung their bats so wildly, they hit each other, at times, without the slightest reaction. They had blood shot eyes, specks of dried blood on cracked lips and they foamed from the mouth as they wailed like banshees barreling at Bubbles and Buttons.

The women came at them so hard and fast, all they could do was try their best to parry the women's strikes and back up against the opposite end of the cage. Marco's gladiators had some help with deflecting the blows by the other two women themselves; their wild swings hitting **each other** was a big plus but occasionally some connected with their intended targets and even though the wild women were rarely hitting Bubbles and Bubbles, those few blows compared to their none, signaled they were losing this fight.

Marco stood with a look of disgust over his fighters being dominated while Joe ran to the edge of the glass with worry etched all over his face.

As the wild women pummeled them with blows from aluminum bats, Buttons looked up at the glass long enough to see Joe watching. The look in his eyes said they were in danger of being killed! At that moment, Buttons decided she was not going to lose that fight or her life.

As she barely fought off her attacker, she chanced a look at Bubbles and saw her in the same situation; *that* pushed her to act and act quickly.

Buttons reached deep inside her dark soul and forced all the rage inside to suddenly explode outward. She handled the bat with both her hands across her body and exploded forward, driving her attacker to the ground. She swung her bat at the head the woman attacking Bubbles and knocked her to the ground as well, leaving behind a mist of blood and teeth.

"Fuck girl...you alright?"Bubbles asked.

"I'm good...just trying to live, they ain't dead yet so we needed to finish them quick before they finish us," Buttons hurriedly said to Bubbles.

As soon as Buttons turned to face her opponent, the woman was already in striking mode and caught her on her left arm before she could fully block. Buttons quickly sidestepped the woman, grabbed the bat with her right hand and cracked her opponent across her face, sending her to the ground a bloody mess.

Bubbles took full advantage of the breathing room Buttons provided her.. before her opponent could get up, she jumped on top of her, violently smashing her opponent's face and head with the end of the bat. The woman screamed, kicked and clawed at Bubbles but fortunately her training had kicked in and she was solely focused on beating the life out of this woman.

Buttons had made her opponent drop her bat and had her pinned against the ground with the bat across her throat crushing her windpipe. The woman kicked, clawed and screamed with what little air she had as her eyes popped from their sockets due to the pressure. Buttons pressed her weight down on the bat with serious intent and squeezed. The woman's efforts to survive slowly deteriorated as blood flooded her brain. Her eyes grew bloodshot and blood began to leak from the sockets, giving new meaning to 'blood tears'. She was bleeding from her ears, nose and mouth as well.

With one last forceful push on the bat, there was a squishing sound and the woman's movements ceased. Once the woman stopped moving and breathing, Buttons sat on top of her, huffing and puffing to catch her breath.

Bubbles was also in full control of her fight as she perched over the woman pummeling her head and face with the broad end of the bat. As she beat the woman, you could hear the sound of her skull cracking under the pressure. Bubbles eventually went into full blood rage, continuing to pummel the woman even after her head cracked open and her brain content spilled out everywhere. Buttons had to go over to Bubbles, grabbing her by the shoulders to get her to finally stop.

Bubbles turned and looked at Buttons with a blank stare then stood up and dropped her bat before screaming...

"Let us out this muthafuckin cage... NOW!!!!!"

In the glass booth Joe had a smile of relief on his face while Marco shook hands with several people, collecting great sums of money from them with a wide grin on his face. He then said something in Russian over the intercom and the armed men opened the cage, escorting Bubbles and Buttons up to the glass booth. When they arrived in the room, everyone was standing in a semi circle, all wearing white face Halloween masks except Marco and Joe.

"Congratulations ladies! That was a great performance. This is my board of directors and they are very pleased to meet you both," Marco said with such pride it was sickening.

The board of directors consisted of twenty people; fifteen men and five women. They were all finely dressed and draped in thousands, maybe millions of dollars worth of jewelry.

"Why is everybody wearing masks," Bubbles asked.

"Because our business is so sensitive, we prefer to keep our identities anonymous. Enough about us... this is your time and we believe you two will be the best champions we've ever had." This came from one of the masked men.

"Get them some champagne please,"

Marco said to Joe. For the first time they could recall, he spoke to the young man in English.

The masked man who'd spoken to earlier began clapping his hands, the rest of the cabinet joining in as Bubbles and Buttons sipped their champagne.

"Take them to the car and wait for me," Marco said to Joe.

****

"Are you two alright?" Joe asked with obvious concern as he grabbed ice bags from the limousine cooler.

"Yeah, we're good except for a few bumps and bruises," Buttons responded painfully as she took a bag of ice and placed it against her forehead.

A few moments later Marco and his board of directors came out of the building;

they all entered separate limousines.

"Here's your payment and I even threw in a little something extra because the board of directors were very pleased with your performance and the ratings were amazing. I have arranged a great feast at the house to celebrate your first televised victory." His words had just the shock effect he was hoping for.

"What the fuck you mean televised performance..."Bubbles harshly responded as she pressed a bag of ice against her shoulder. "...what kinda bullshit are you up to know Marco?!"

"Oh, did I not mention your performances are televised to select clients around the world. Not only are you two great warriors but you are becoming famous among the world's elite. Isn't that great news... "He wore the most innocently sadistic smile imaginable.

"I don't really care about being famous because we were kind of famous at home before and that was alright but right now we're more concerned with being paid well and living long enough to enjoy it," Bubbles replied sarcastically.

As they drove towards home, Marco grabbed some cigars from an arm ready console and handed one to each of them, including Joe, before responding to Bubbles.

"You will get a chance to enjoy your wealth and fame if you continue to win and follow my rules. "

When they arrived home that night, they laughed, drank and ate while Bubbles and Buttons found out more about Marco's obsession with his rules and orders being followed to the letter.

During the celebration, Marco told one of his servers to fetch a special bottle of wine he'd wanted chilled. Unfortunately the server had not been told to put the bottle on chill by one of his personal assistants. When the server told Marco the message was not passed to him, Marco became infuriated and yelled for the assistant he'd originally given the order.The assistant had obviously been briefed on why he was being called because he arrived visibly worried.

"Did I not tell you to make sure the bottle of wine was chilling to celebrate in case my girls won?"

The assistant started to reply in Russian but Marco stopped him.

"I asked you in English so I expect you to respond the same. "

"Yes...yes sir...I sorry," the guy responded in broken English. "I had to...to run an er...rand for my mother and I...I must have forgots. "

"Oh, you ran an errand for your mother? And how is she? "

"She...she does well sir and she...she always asks of your well being. Thanks for...for asking sir," the guy responded with a modest smile.

"I'm glad to hear that ...I must send her a card to express my condolences on her loss."

"Her...her loss sir? There are no recent tragedies in...in our family that I know of," the guy answered with a puzzled look on his face.

"Oh you didn't hear, she recently lost a son," Marco said with a stone cold stare in his eyes.

The guy processed Marco's words in his head and his puzzled look quickly turned to one of abject fear.

"Sir...sir please no," the guy said followed by a string of hurried words in Russian.

Marco then laughed, "I am not going to kill you...but he is." He pointed to the server he'd told to get the wine from the refrigerator.

The assistant bolted from the room towards the door. Marco quickly grabbed a walkie-talkie from his side and yelled orders in Russian. After a few seconds, he received a reply over the radio and moments later three heavily armed men came into the room dragging the terrified assistant.

"You really going to kill him over a simple bottle of wine," Bubbles asked.

"Of course not... why would I take someone's life over a bottle of wine. He will die because he did not follow my orders."

Bubbles then stood up, "we've had enough of that for today...we're going to bed."

"SIT THE FUCK DOWN, YOU WILL HAVE ENOUGH WHEN I SAY YOU'VE HAD ENOUGH," Marco barked.

Bubbles slowly took her seat as Marco ordered his armed guards to put the assistant down on his knees in front of them.

"You're really going to do this right here right now," Buttons uttered.

With toughened lips, Marco turned towards Buttons, giving her a stare which gave her a non-verbal command to shut the fuck up.

The assistant had started crying and speaking rapidly in Russian; no doubt pleading for his life. Marco then reached his hands out and one of his armed guards placed a pistol in it. He handed the pistol to the terrified server who hesitantly took it. The server stood still for a few seconds staring at the weapon now resting in his hands.

"What are you waiting for? Kill him or you will take his place and we will see what happens when the gun is in his hands," Marco told the server.

The server took a long look at Marco then turned his attention to the assistant. He raised the gun to the man's head with a shaky hand, closed his eyes and pulled the trigger.

BAM!

The back of the assistant's head exploded, spewing bone and brain fragments all over the place before his body fell to the floor like a sack of potatoes. The server then slowly lowered his hand as smoke rose from the barrel of the pistol and the smell of gunpowder and death filled the room.

"Now that wasn't so bad was it," Marco said to the still in shock server as he took the pistol from his hand. The server just stood silent looking down at the blood pouring from the head of the man he had just killed.

Marco looked at Bubbles and Buttons and just shook his head.

BAM!!

Marco killed the server and his body fell next to the assistant.

"Now you may go," Marco said as he shouted commands to Joe and left the room.

That night. Marco sent a message that was well received by Bubbles and Buttons...it was his way or death.

As the weeks passed, Bubbles and Buttons fought for their lives inside and outside of the cage. Everyday they grew closer to promised freedom and wealth with death constantly at their hands and in their minds.

Each fight became more brutal and violent as Marco and his board members brainstormed different unconventional and deadly means of providing the entertainment of human butchery to their fetish crazed and twisted audiences.

4

BREAKING POINT

The intense fighting transformed Bubbles and Buttons from Sultry seductresses to Deadly Divas. Bubbles developed a hunger for money and power while Buttons developed her talent for pain. They both also developed their own personal relationship with Joe. Bubbles found a little brother while Buttons found something more intimate.

It is now week five, which means Bubbles and Buttons are half way through their deal with Marco.

Bubbles, Buttons and Joe were eating lunch in the dining room a few hours before their fifth televised performance when Marco walked into the room.

"You two have made me very proud and very wealthy. You have bested some dangerous opponents with bats, knives, hooks, whips and bamboo and your bare hands. Tonight will be something special, the weapon of choice is the meat cleaver and in order to win you must fully decapitate your opponents with nothing left between the head and torso... how exciting is that?! "

"Exciting for you and your nutty ass friends but our assess will be fighting *not* to get our heads chopped the fuck off," Bubbles replied.

"I don't think we have to worry about that...once they give them that hot shot they fight hard but they don't think. We just have to make sure we stay alive and in one piece," Buttons arrogantly said.

Marco just laughed and left the room.

"What's so funny" Bubbles yelled at his retreating figure but got no response from him.

"He's probably laughing because we are making him very fucking wealthy... like he said while we get paid pennies."

"Pennies...we've made over thirty thousand dollars. You call that pennies?" Buttons replied.

"Compared to what we could make... yes. You must get paid well huh lil Joe? You always seem to have money," Bubbles said.

"Marco gives me money every now and then but mostly because of who Marco is I have no need of money."

"Sounds good but with seeing all the

money and power Marco has, don't you ever want some of it for yourself," Bubbles asked.

"What Marco has, he built, and I feel if the same is meant for me it will come. In this business greed can get you killed or worse."

"Enough talking about nothing, come on and sneak off camera with me and beat this pussy up before this fight," Buttons sensually demanded of Joe. Knowing the locations of the cameras throughout the house was a major plus when Joe and Buttons began the physical side of their relationship. He would take her to blind spots throughout the house so they could sex each other the right way.

:Let's go in the bathroom," Joe said.

He grabbed her hand, looked up at the

two cameras in the corners of the ceiling and zigzagged his way to the bathroom.

"You know the routine... Bubbles keep an eye out. " He winked at her.

Bubbles winked back as he and Buttons disappeared.

The bathroom was as elegant as every other room in the house. It featured his and hers sinks, a garden Jacuzzi jet tub and marble and stainless steel everywhere.

Both were hot and ready for some heavy duty fucking that always took place when they came together. Joe's nine inch dick swelled and fought to escape his pants while Buttons' bulky breasts and large nipples push the buttons on her blouse close to their limits.

Joe sported a five nine, one hundred eighty pound muscled frame and he put every ounce of it into hoisting Buttons up as a wet spot formed on her jeans in between her legs.

"Oohh Joe," she moaned.

Joe carried her over to the dry tub and gently placed her down in it. He quickly stripped off his clothing and unselfishly ignored his stiffness to tend to Buttons' sticky wet spot. He pulled down her jeans and stripped her lust soaked silk panties carefully with his teeth to tease her of his intentions. He went to his knees, spread her thighs and dove his face into her wet and warm opening. Using his pointer finger and thumb, Joe spread the lips of her pussy and began to lap up her sweet juices like a kid lapping ice cream from a cone.

While Joe hungrily feasted on Buttons'

pussy banquet, her body arched and stiffened as she gripped his head holding him in place and released a gush of love juice into his mouth and face.

"Uhmmm..." she moaned.

Buttons then righted herself and laid Joe on his back for his turn to be orally pleasured. She crawled on top of him like a leopard stalking prey, eyeing her nine inch prize throbbing with anticipation. She locked her palms around the robust shaft and took him deep into her warm moist mouth.

Joe's toes curled and rocked his body with the pleasure he received from the insertion.   "Uhmmm..."

Buttons vigorously swallowed Joe's swollen dick for a few minutes before she positioned herself on top of him to take all nine deep inside her. He watched her with bedroom eyes as she gripped the sides of the tub and slowly lowered herself onto his awaiting rod. Her neck stiffened and her head went back as his dick penetrated the swollen lips of her wanting pussy.

After a few slow strokes to fit his dick precisely, she began to ride him at a steady. pleasing pace.

KNOCK...KNOCK

"Time to start wrapping it up," Bubbles said through the door.

Their next performance was in two hours and Bubbles knew Marco liked to leave early and she did her best to keep their secret kept. Bubbles figured keeping Joe happy would greatly benefit her when it was time for her to make her power play.

A few minutes after Bubbles knocked,

the bathroom door eased open and Buttons and Joe slowly and carefully made their way into the room.

"I almost lost track of time messing around with you..." Joe whispered to Buttons as he smiled shyly. "...I'm going to see if Marco is ready..." He fixed his clothing while bolting from the room.

"That good fucking got me hungry... let's go see if it's not too late to get something to eat," Buttons said.

Bubbles looked at her and laughed as they made their way to the kitchen. When they reached it, Marco had just finished eating and was getting up from the table.

"Good.. you're here... perfect timing. I was going to send for you after this quick snack. "

"I'm kind of hungry myself. Do we

have time to grab something to eat? We still have an hour and fifteen minutes," Buttons pleaded.

"Alright..get something quick and meet me at the car."

They grabbed a quick sandwich, hurried to the car and left for the arena.

****

When they arrived, as usual Marco and Joe were escorted to the high glass room while Bubbles and Buttons were led to the cage. Inside, there were several meat cleavers hanging from the bars in various spots. Within minutes, another set of armed men appeared escorting two large and heavily tattooed women to the cage.

"Ladies and gentleman, with this being mid-season into our program and these two fighters being the best we ever

had surviving this long, tonight's performance will be even more dangerous and brutal instead of the usual crazed wild women. I will adjust the dose of my fight formula enough for them to perform intelligently," Marco said over a loudspeaker.

These two women were larger than usual but they still were lethargic slumps like their other opponents. The import of Marco's words hadn't quite sunk in with Bubbles and Buttons, but it would before this fight night was done.

Marco yelled something in Russian over the loudspeaker and after positioning the women in the cage, one of the armed men walked into the cage, administered the injection and quickly exited the cage locking it behind him.

Joe, Bubbles and Buttons

With the understanding of Marco's announcement now dawning, Bubbles and Buttons stood in shock and fear of facing something more deadly than they ever had in the previous fights. Bubbles grabbed Buttons' hand and pulled her backwards towards the cage and the cleavers, all the while keeping a steady eye on their opponents.

When Bubbles grabbed her hand, Buttons knew instinctively to follow her lead. They reached the back side of the cage, grabbed cleavers tightly in their hands and faced the opposition head on.

The other two slowly straightened their bodies, grabbed their heads and began screaming to high hell. They both then dropped to the ground and laid still for a while. Bubbles and Buttons relaxed their stances at the sight of the women on the ground...but it was momentary.

The board members jumped from their seats and stared at Marco with worried expressions, while Marco sat confidently in his chair.

"Look," he said, pointing towards the cage.

The board members turned their attention back to center stage just as the women started to stir. They slowly rose to their feet, looking around them in bewilderment. Each looked around the cage in wonderment as Bubbles and Buttons returned to combat mode.

"WHAT THE FUCK IS GOING ON HERE," one of the women yelled in a strong Latin accent.

Marco again yelled a command in

Russian to his armed men around the cage and they all trained their weapons on the two. He then addressed the woman's question rather matter-of-factly.

"All you need to know is that you are in a fight to the death, either you kill them, they kill you or those men kill you...quite simply the choice is yours."

"You can't do this to us,"the other woman voiced. She too had a Latin accent.

Marco yelled another command in Russian and the armed men readied their machine guns, unleashed a small flurry of lead into the cage and the bullets ripped through the smaller of the two women, sending her to the ground in a smoking heap.

Everyone looked on in horror except Marco, whose facial expression stayed hard and firm while the woman's body twitched on the ground, her blood coating the surface of the cage.

"You are a fucking monster," Bubbles yelled out.

"Call me what you want but if any of you want to live, I better see some fucking fighting right fucking now," Marco furiously demanded over the loudspeaker as he banged his fist on the table.

"Oh...so now it's two on one... it don't seem fair to me," Bubbles yelled sarcastically.

A large and sinister smirk slowly formed on Marco's face..

"That's one thing you're right about, so why don't you wait outside the cage while your friend fights her."

"HELL TO THE NO...THAT'S NOT

FAIR! SHE'S DOUBLE BUBBLES' SIZE.. WHY CAN'T I FIGHT HER," Buttons screamed adamantly.

"You can't because I said you can't... why do you think that bitch is dead on the ground now? I am god here and what I say goes, I thought you had already learned this lesson but I see I was wrong so I will give you an absolute lesson. Only one of you will leave here tonight or neither of you will. You will fight the winner of this match!"

"FUCK YOU MARCO! WE TOLD YOU WE WILL NEVER FIGHT EACH OTHER AND IF YOU KILL US OFF WHAT ABOUT YOUR AUDIENCE, RATINGS AND MONEY," Bubbles angrily responded.

"I was successful before you and I will

be successful after you," Marco replied. He then shouted orders in Russian over the loudspeaker. The armed men opened the cage, forcing Buttons out by gunpoint as they exchanged looks of worry.

"If I gotta die anyway, why should I fight her instead of just letting you kill me," Bubbles' opponent asked Marco.

"Great question.... how does this sound? If you win, I will have your criminal record wiped clean and I will pay you a hundred thousand dollars. "

"Man please...How do I know you're not lying to me and won't just kill me if I win or not?"

"We are being watched by thousands around the world so I not only made that promise to you but to them also... look."

Marco then pointed to the ceiling and

all the cameras mounted in various positions. The woman looked the cameras, back at Bubbles then quickly ran to grab a meat cleaver from the cage bars. She faced Bubbles in a fighting stance; Bubbles matched her move.

"That's the idea but before you start there are some ground rules, no one does anything until I give the command to fight and the winner can only win by holding up the head of the loser," Marco added.

"**FIGHT!**" he yelled.

The woman yelled and rushed Bubbles with the cleaver raised. Bubbles easily sidestepped her, swung and slashed her across the back.

"Arrrr," the woman yelled in pain but she quickly shrugged it off, grabbing Bubbles by her throat and slamming her against the cage, causing her to drop her cleaver. The woman swung down at Bubbles but she grabbed her wrist and struggled to keep her at bay.

This woman stood a good six foot six or seven easily, towering over Bubbles *and* Buttons. The woman's size and strength was almost overwhelming for Bubbles. As she pressed her attack, Bubbles legs began to weaken and tremble.

Seeing her friend at a serious disadvantage, Buttons, under armed guard, shouted out "FIGHT BUBBLES! YOU BETTER FUCKING FIGHT! "

When it came to winning a fight with overwhelming size and strength, Buttons was well suited for it but unfortunately it was Bubbles in the cage with a beast of a woman. Bubbles had a furious fighting spirit; while pinned against the cage and struggling to keep a meat cleaver from splitting her scalp, she punched and kicked at the woman as much as she could but to no avail. The big bitch hardly flinched from the blows, staying intent on splitting her wide open.

In order to save her life, Bubbles made a desperate move. She dropped all her weight to the ground and as the woman leaned down still gripping her, Bubbles kicked her in the face. The kick stunned the woman long enough for Bubbles to grab the meat cleaver she had dropped.

CLINK...

"AAHHH!!!" Bubbles screamed as the woman slammed her meat cleaver down on Bubbles' right hand, sending blood squirting and three fingers rolling across the cage. Somehow, after absorbing the intense pain, Bubbles managed to swing her cleaver, slicing into the woman's Achilles. As the woman curled back in pain, Bubbles took the opportunity to get back to her feet and on the offensive.

The woman screamed in pain, struggling to get to her feet as Bubbles took a moment to tend to her injury. She quickly tore away a piece of her top to wrapped her mangled hand. By the time she finished, her opponent was back on her feet and armed with a meat cleaver in both hands. Due to her injury she was only able to use one of her legs so she slightly hopped about the cage with her teeth clenched and death in her eyes.

Bubbles had lost the use of one hand;

however, she had mobility on her side and she knew it. So she slowly stalked her like a predator stalking prey, keeping her off balance by making quick side to side movements. As Bubbles closed in on her, she would wildly strike at her and hobble back to keep Bubbles in front of her.

Unable to penetrate the woman's defenses with a frontal attack, Bubbles chose another strategy. The entire cage was spotted with about twenty meat cleavers, so Bubbles decided to use them along with her mobility to hopefully win the fight. She crept as close to her opponent as she could while staying out of her strike range and pitched her meat cleaver at her. The woman barely dodged Bubbles' attack and the cleaver flew past her head banged off a cage bar and onto the ground. Bubbles then quickly raced to another cleaver and repeated her action with better success. This time the cleaver spiked into her left shoulder. The woman screamed from the impact and dropped the cleaver in her left hand.

The sight of the knife in the woman's shoulder and blood leaking pleased Bubbles. With a sly smile on her face and another cleaver in her hand, Bubbles confidently bounced back and forth ready to attack again. The woman, on the other hand, was faced with a dangerous decision because the cleaver in her shoulder was slowly sapping her blood and strength and she could not use her left arm. She could either fight with the cleaver in her shoulder and one arm possibly bleeding to death or drop the cleaver in her right hand to remove the cleaver in her shoulder and leave herself vulnerable to attack. Oh but life is so full of hard decisions!

The woman gazed at Bubbles, tracking her every movement. She clenched her teeth, dropped her cleaver, reached for the one in her shoulder and yanked it out. Bubbles paused, straightened and stared at the woman as she stood huffing and puffing with blood leaking from her left shoulder and a bloody cleaver raised in her right hand.

"Come on you bitch... that's all you got," the woman said as she reached down and picked up the meat cleaver she dropped with her left hand.

"Oh no bitch... there's plenty more where that came from," Bubbles responded. She raised her arm to launch another knife when the woman lunged at her quickly, hopping on one leg. The woman's brave attack surprised Bubbles and she slightly delayed before dodging, which got her slashed in the face. Even though the attack caught Bubbles off guard, she still buried her meat cleaver deep in the woman's back between her shoulder blades. The woman stumbled to the ground from the blow and Buttons immediately jumped her, leaning her weight into driving the cleaver deeper into the woman's body The woman struggled with all her might to get Bubbles off her back but the blood lust in Bubbles boiled to the surface as she violently grunted while forcing her blade into the woman's body as the blood erupted.

Suddenly there was a cracking sound

that echoed throughout the room and the woman instantly stopped moving. Bubbles' blade penetrated her spine and immediately paralyzed her, yet Bubbles kept pushing down on the blade.

Seeing the end of the fight near, Marco's stone face softened to a satisfied grin at seeing his creation at work. After a while of unleashing her fury on her lifeless opponent, Bubbles suddenly ended her attack. Covered in her opponent's blood and breathing heavily, she slowly stood up and started to walk to the cage door.

"You can not leave the cage until the job is done in full," Marco blasted over the loudspeaker.

Bubbles froze in her steps, looked up at Marco and silently walked over to her opponent. With her one good arm, she grabbed her opponent by her right arm and dragged her to the center of the cage leaving behind a blood trail. After such an intense battle, Bubbles had forgotten the stipulations Marco put on winning the fight but now that he reminded her she was going to give him what he wanted. She put her foot down on her opponent's back, grabbed the handle of the cleaver jammed in so deep only the handle showed and yanked it out, slinging blood and flesh about the cage.

"IS THIS WHAT YOU FUCKING WANT....IS THIS WHAT YOU FUCKING WANT!!!!!," she screamed as she looked up at Marco. She then knelt down and started forcefully hacking at her opponent's neck. Everyone just watched straight faced and silently as Bubbles made a mess of the cage.

After continuous wild hackings, the woman's head finally separated from her body and rolled awkwardly in a pool of blood. Struggling to catch her breath, Bubbles grabbed her opponent's severed head, stood up and threw it outside the cage.

"Now you get me the hell out of here and to a fucking hospital...you twisted bastard! "

The armed men looked up at Marco and Marco nodded his head signaling to let Bubbles out of the cage.

****

The ride home that night was very awkward. Instead of Marco sitting in the back with them drinking and celebrating, he sat up front quietly with the driver. Joe sat in back, tending to Bubbles' injuries.

"We're going to the hospital aren't we? I lost a lot of blood and I'm not feeling so good?" Bubbles asked.

"We aren't going to the hospital.. we're going back to the house. We have equipment to be able to take care of you there," Joe responded.

When they arrived back at the house, Marco quickly hopped out the limousine and disappeared inside.

"What's stuck up his ass," Buttons asked Joe.

"He's mad that you two are still alive... he thinks that you are challenging him too much."

"Are you serious?! He's mad that we're still alive after everything he put us through! That muthafucka had the nerve to be mad at the fact we're the best and we know it," Bubbles furiously responded as she stumbled slightly weak from blood loss.

Joe and Buttons quickly grabbed her by the arms and led her into the house.

"We have a doctor on call twenty-four hours... let's take her into the kitchen..."

"Marco really didn't want you two to survive tonight's performance but the woman he killed ruined his plans by questioning him so much. He was going to have you all killed but the chairman of the board wants to see at least one more fight with you two because of the ratings you bring..."

Buttons took this moment to interrupt Joe...

"And...who is this chairman of the board that saved our lives?" Buttons asked Joe as they walked into the kitchen.

"You've met him personally before... Mr. Andre."

Bubbles stopped in her tracks and looked Joe in the eye...

"You mean that fat muthafucka who wanted us to beat him while he ate our pussy. "

"Yeah, that's him," Joe replied.

Joe took them to another room in the house similar to a hospital emergency room. He yelled in Russian into a back room and this little old man waddled out.

"Who the fuck is that," Bubbles asked impatiently. The blood loss was making her dizzy and the pain was coming back with a vengeance. If something wasn't done soon, she go into shock.

"This is our resident physician. He lives in the house and he has been our doctor ever since I can remember. He is very good, so let him help you." Joe was very gentle with her.

The old man directed Bubbles to sit on a table, grabbing her mangled hand wrapped in bloody cloth. He slowly unwrapped the make-shift bandage to inspect the severity of the injury.

"Oh shit... you better be careful old man." Bubbles whispered with trepidation. *This shit is really starting to hurt* she spoke in her mind, not willing to show any weakness.

The old doctor washed her mangled hand in an antiseptic bath, poured some type of sterilizer like alcohol on it, rubbed antibiotic cream all over the wounds then wrapped it in fresh bandages. He checked her other injuries, cleansing and treating them in the same fashion then disappeared as quickly as he'd appeared. He materialized once again as if by magic with three pills, instructing Bubbles to "take these...an antibiotic for infection and 2 pain relievers..." And just like that...Poof...he was gone.

"Damn this feels a lot better even though I lost some of my muthafuckin fingers... So is Marco going to try and kill us," Bubbles asked Joe as she gently inspected her neatly wrapped hand.

Joe was a bit hesitant in responding. He knew the price to be paid for any disloyalty or disobedience to Marco but his love/lust for Buttons got the better of him...

"He was very upset that you were injured and didn't die. I heard him and the board talking about fighting you two against each other for the next fight..."

"What if we don't fight..." Buttons interrupted him yet again. "...what will they do if we refuse to fight one another?"

"He's planning to kill you two off camera and make up some type of brutal story to make your deaths entertaining. He's already planned another trip to go scouting again."

"So he's really gonna to kill us.... what do we do now," Buttons asked Bubbles. All their suspicions were confirmed; this had been Marco's plan all along. He never intended to let them leave here alive!

"We'll talk about that later... right now

I just want to get some rest if you don't mind Joe," Bubbles responded. She was no longer sure Joe could be trusted.

"Sure, no problem. I will let you two get some rest. I have to check in with Marco anyway," Joe gave Buttons a tender kiss and headed off.

"I know this shit is fucked up but don't forget Joe has always been in our corner Bubbles..." Buttons had correctly interpreted her concern and couldn't imagine Joe would betray them.

"I know he's always helped us but shit is real now... even though you fucking him, we don't really know just how loyal to Marco he is..." Shit had really come down to life or death and Bubbles just wasn't willing to take chances with their lives that could easily lead to their deaths.

Joe, Bubbles and Buttons

That night, Bubbles laid out a plan that would either grant them their freedom or cost them their lives. They had just fought and weren't scheduled to fight until next week so whatever they were going to do they had a week to do it and do it right.

****

The next morning Bubbles, Buttons and Joe ate breakfast at their usual time but Marco was unusually late. When he finally arrived, he was dressed in a sharp Italian suit, similar to what he wore when they met him, rushing for the door. He turned to look at them as though they were an afterthought before replying...

"I almost forgot about this meeting... I have to fly out and I will not be returning until next Friday, right before your next performance. Andre will be staying over until I return." Marco lowered his brow and squinted his eyes with intimidation at the three of them, "I expect no problems," he added on his way out the door.

"I can't believe it...a whole six days without his uptight ass. I know he's going to recruit more girls but this is also our time to plan our escape," Bubbles uttered, fixing her eyes on Joe to judge his reaction.

Joe looked at them with sadness in his face and in resonated in his voice, "you're planning an escape?"

Buttons walked over to him and pressed his face deeply into her bosom as she hugged him, "Yeah baby, we have no choice but to escape or die and I know you know that too... "

Joe, Bubbles and Buttons

"He did say something about you two becoming more and more defiant each time you win." Joe looked close to tears.

Bubbles walked over to put a hand on Joe's shoulder.

"You do know when we go you are more than welcome to come with us."

Joe began to shake his head in the negative...

"I will miss you both greatly, especially you Buttons, but my place is here with Marco for now..."

"What?! I love you Joe and I thought you loved me too," Buttons countered, her sadness matching his.

Joe placed his hand gently on Buttons' cheek..

"You are my first love and you will always have a place in my heart but this is my life and I'm not ready to leave it. I will give you all the help you need but I can't go with you. "

A single tear fell as she tenderly kissed him, "I understand...thank you for everything and I will never forget you."

"There will be plenty of time for goodbyes later ...right now we have to figure out how we're going to do this without getting you into any trouble," Bubbles said to Joe, her heart breaking at the thought of leaving him at the mercy of the monster.

While they talked in the kitchen, the doorbell rang. As always, one of the servants answered and seconds later Andre walked into the room, "my friends it's good to see you again."

"It's good to see you too Andre and

thanks for getting us out of that bind Mr. Chairman of the board," Bubbles said.

"You two have been the greatest warriors we've ever had and I could not stand to see you go down in such a dishonorable fashion."

"You think there is anything honorable about her fighting at all with a fucked up hand," Buttons asked Andre heatedly.

"It is a sad thing, her injury, but that is part of this business. Unfortunately, you're going to have to make do with what you have," Andre answered as he took a seat at the table and lit a cigarette. "Well since I'm here and we have all this time to kill, how about we have a little fun. " His eyes held that sadistic twinkle in anticipation of his version of "the pleasure principle."

"We'll beat your crazy ass damn near

to death if you want if in return you let us go while Marco is away," Bubbles said to Andre in a serious and frustrated tone.

"Sorry my dear but it don't work like that. Even though I was able to spare your lives for but a moment, you can only escape death by winning out. When Marco started this great organization he did so for my pleasure and entertainment while he was a prisoner himself. Not only did everyone enjoy it but we made lots of money and..."

Bubbles forcefully interjected, "if it's about the fucking money, Marco is going out right now to get girls to replace us and your money still rolls in... why force us to fight anymore. We have blood on our hands too so you don't have to worry about us going to any law enforcement. That shit would be real stupid on our part, don't ya think..."

Andre laughed.

"That's the least of our worries. The thing is, you were born in the cage on the cameras and that's where you will ensure yourselves a long future or die. That is the nature of this business...I like you two but there will always be more and more and more just like you... "

"You feel like that and you want us to satisfy your sick fantasies you fat muthafucka!" Bubbles was beside herself with anger and frustration. She hated them all and what they had forced them to do and forced them to become...almost less than human.

Andre slammed his fist down on the

table, "how dare you talk to me like that you stupid bitch!!! You should be on your fucking knees thanking me for sparing your lives even to this moment."

A long hard stillness arose in the room as Bubbles, Buttons and Andre exchanged dirty looks. Joe sensed the tension, his instincts telling him to intervene before something fucked up happened but before he could.. act it happened.

Bubbles got up as if she was leaving the kitchen. Hearing a fat fuck like Andre disrespect her and Buttons after everything they'd been put through, up to and including her becoming maimed, was more than she could take...she had definitely had enough!

NO MORE...

5

On The Run

The fire Marco had forged inside of Bubbles only stoked during intense combat but that all changed in one instance. Just as Bubbles crossed the threshold of the kitchen to the hallway, she bolted back to the table, grabbed a butter knife from the breakfast meal still smeared with butter and jabbed it so hard intro Andre's throat his flesh exploded open. His eyes burst open from the force of the death blow as his life blood erupted and gushed from the hole in his throat.

Joe and Buttons froze in their conversation, their eyes widened and their jaws dropped at the sight of a blood drench

Bubbles standing over the body of Marco's Chairman of the Board.

Joe quickly grabbed Andre's side pistol and pointed it at Bubbles and Buttons...

"WHAT THE FUCK DID YOU DO THAT FOR?" Joe released the the safety, "BOTH OF YOU GET AGAINST THE FUCKING WALL! "

"Calm down baby, I love you...I won't do anything to you and let anything happen to you," Bubbles said softly, slowly walk towards him while Bubbles stood motionless trying to catch her breath.

"I SAID GET THE FUCK AGAINST THE WALL," Joe yelled, with a shaky hand and the pistol held high.

"Ok, just be calm baby... no one is

going to hurt you. Ain't that right Bubbles," Buttons spoke as calm as she could, while pulling Bubbles close to her.

"I can't believe you killed him...he was my family..."

In tears of anger and hurt, Joe walked toward Andre's lifeless body, while keeping the pistol trained on Bubbles and Buttons, and kissed him on his forehead, "rest my friend."

Bubbles suddenly broke her silence, I'm sorry Joe..."I just couldn't take anymore. After losing my fingers and now have to worry about getting killed for not wanting to kill my best friend... I lost it. I killed him so shoot me if you want, just let Buttons go. " She sank into the nearest chair, trying tired for the first time in her life and just wanting the nightmare to be over.

"We can all leave here right now and go away somewhere forever and leave all this shit behind baby," Buttons pleaded.

With the back of his gun hand, Joe wiped tears from his face, turned and gazed at Bubbles and Buttons...

"Only because I love her will I let you two go but you have to leave now and disappear. When Marco gets back, I will tell him what happened and he will do everything in his power to hunt you down and kill you both. And believe me, he will make it as painful as possible..."

"What do you..."

Before Buttons could finish, Joe held his hand up to stop her.

"My love for you is the only reason you two are still alive, so while there is some left, I suggest you leave. I will instruct the driver to take you to the airport; you're on your own from there."

Buttons slowly walked towards him. opening her arms to embrace him but he extended his arms outward, shaking his head no...

"You'd best get as much as you can while I call the driver. "He then walked out the kitchen.

Buttons stood watching Joe leave and began to cry. Bubbles put her arm around her shoulders...

"I know and I'm sorry but we have to get our things and get the hell out of here."

Buttons looked Bubbles in her eyes and slapped the hell out of her!

"It didn't have to go this way... "

The blow knocked Bubbles to the

ground. Bubbles rose to her feet, rubbed her sore face and followed Buttons to their room.

****

They didn't have many personal belongings but they did have a hundred thousand dollars saved between the both of them. Bubbles and Buttons quickly and quietly packed their things without exchanging one glance or whisper. Once they finished they quickly headed for the door. When they stepped outside, there was Joe standing in the snow flurries next to a limousine with the door open and a stone cold stare on his face.

Bubbles headed for the car first. As she went to get in, she forced a quick hug on Joe and slid in. Buttons sadly made her way into the car. She was caught completely off guard when Joe grabbed her by the arm and yanked her into his then gave her a deep and passionate kiss melting her in his arms. He disengaged and looked deep into her eyes...

"I'm sorry things turned out this way. "

"Me too," Buttons exclaimed, as she eyed Bubbles sitting in the limousine. With a final wave goodbye, they drove away.

****

Once Bubbles and Buttons vanished from sight, Joe went back into the house heart broken and distressed. Not only did he lose the first woman he'd ever loved but now he had to face cleaning up the dead body of his beloved friend Andre and even worst than this, breaking the news to Marco. As he stood in emotional pain over Andre's body, he pulled out his cell phone, his hand trembled as he dialed the numbers. The phone rang and Marco answered...

"Hello? "

While riding to the airport, the two women sat self-absorbed, not wanting any contact with the other. Regardless of what happened or how it happened, they were deep in this shit together and they both knew it. Along with the fact that they had to trust each other if they expected to survive.

Bubbles decided to break the tension filled silence...

"I know this shit is all my fault and I'm so sorry for everything. If you want, when we get to the airport, we'll go our separate ways."

Buttons slowly turned her head, reluctantly facing Bubbles.

"Yeah, you fucked up big time but... like I said before, we got into this mess together and we'll get out of it the same way."

They forced smiles on their faces and hugged just as the limousine stopped. The driver rolled down the dividing window with a pistol in his hand, speaking to them in heavily accented English...

"This is where you get out!"

Neither had expected to be forced from the car at gun point so fear raced in their minds as they wondered if they were really being driven to the airport or some deserted wasteland where they would be left for dead or executed. Due to the intense snowfall, all they could see through the window was the appearance of a deserted building in a snow covered field.

"Where are we...we were told we're going to the airport but this don't look like no airport," Bubbles said, truly fed up with the whole game being played out in front of them.

The driver removed the safety, "I said this is where you get out! "

"Okay...okay... we're going," Bubbles said.

They opened the door and stepped out into the frozen tundra with their things and started to walk towards the building. No sooner than they were a few feet from the car, it took off, leaving them in the middle of nowhere.

"If this is where it all ends, at least we're here together," Buttons said as they walked towards the building. They walked up to two metal doors that suddenly opened to the sight of a private aircraft hanger. There was a mid size plane sitting there with a guy standing next to it waiting.

"Let's go... I...I ave a deed line," the guy barked in broken English.

Bubbles and Buttons made their way onto the plane.

"Where you go...now "the guy asked.

"The United States... Florida" Bubbles responded.

Before they took off, Buttons asked the pilot if she could use his phone to make a quick call. Of course, when he gave her his phone, she called Lil Joe.

"Hello? "

"Hey Joe... this is Buttons. I just wanted to call to say thanks again for everything, are you going to be alright?"

"Why are you calling me from a Russian number?! You should be on a plane out of the country right now."

"We are on the plane Joe, I just wanted to talk to you one last time and I hope the stupid actions of Bubbles don't get you in any trouble with Marco. "

"Things are what they are now. I told Marco what happened and you know he now wants you two or your heads delivered to him. He has assassins all over the world and they all are now hunting for you."

"Well just know I love you Joe and will always keep you in my heart. "

"I...."

Just as Joe was about to answer, the line went dead as the plane left Russian airspace.

"Hello...hello...Joe?"

Not receiving an answer, she looked at the cell phone and her heart dropped at the sight of no antenna bars. She handed the pilot his phone and asked, "how long will this trip take?"

"You say you want go to Floreda in the United Sates then it take fifteen hours. There be sleeping quarters in back if you want sleep. "

"Ok"

Buttons went to where Bubbles was sitting and they went back to the sleeping area where they both just went to sleep. It was like a rest much needed after what they left behind but it was also rest to prepare for what was to come. They figured Marco was a powerful man with many resources but they really realized his capabilities when they arrived at an airport in Miami Florida.

****

The plane landed at the Miami International Airport. The pilot woke Bubbles and Buttons and they picked up their things to exit the plane. When the side door opened, the two looked at each other with smiles of joy at being back home. They literally jumped off the plane and ran into the airport full of euphoria. As they reached the doors, they were approached by several police officers.

"What's the problem officers?"

Bubbles nervously asked.

One of the policeman had two pictures in his hands, he raised them up and they were pictures of Bubbles and Buttons. The police officers then grabbed Bubbles and Buttons, placed them in handcuffs, put them in two separate police cars and drove to the Miami Police Department.

When they arrived at police headquarters, they were ushered to an interrogation room by a column of police officers.

"WHAT THE HELL ARE YOU DOING... WE HAVEN'T DONE ANYTHING, Bubbles shouted as she struggled with the officers. The officers slammed them down in chairs, shackled them and left the room.

"You think they... "

"Shh.... Don't say anything until we find out something," Bubbles whispered to Buttons.

Moments later, a woman and man dressed in suits walked into the room with folders in their hands. The woman grabbed a chair and sat at the table while the man closed the door behind them and leaned up against the two way mirror eagle eyeing Bubbles and Buttons.

As soon as the woman sat down, she opened her folder and began to slam pictures of dead bodies on the table along with one of Andre.

"We already have you fingerprints and witness statements so the only thing that can help you two monsters is a confession."

Their eyes bulged and jaws dropped at

the sight of the pictures; they both knew Marco had fucked them. Twenty-four hours had not even passed since they left and now they were back under his control, but how?

Bubbles stiffened up in her chair, "we don't know a goddamn thing so if you're going to do something then just do it!"

"Nothing from either of you. You do realized you two are being charged with multiple murder including the murder of a Russian government official. You are wanted by several governments of your victims and they all want to see you two dead..." This came from the woman; the man remained silent through out the entire interrogation.

Bubbles and Buttons kept silent with poker faces...

"We want a lawyer," Bubbles nonchalantly voiced.

The woman read them their Miranda rights and quickly picked up the pictures. She got up from her seat and they left the room. A group of police officers then entered the room to escort Bubbles and Buttons to a room where they were stripped, searched and handed prison jumpers. They were then escorted to a waiting transport van and driven away.

The Florida State Maximum Security Correctional Institute was alive with activity as they prepared to receive the two most wanted women in the known world..Bubbles and Buttons.

Joe, Bubbles and Buttons

News agencies from around the world flocked to the prison to report the capture of the reported international thrill killers, as they were dubbed. When the transport van arrived, a force of corrections officers had to usher the van through a sea of people and camera flashes.

Once they were inside the prison, Bubbles and Buttons were lead to a private room where they were told they would meet with their attorney. Buttons turned to Bubbles with concern on her face, "how are we going to get out of this?"

"I really can't tell you right now or at least until we find out how much they know. Then we can decide what to say and what to do. I know this shit is getting deeper and scarier but we must trust and stand with each other to keep our freedom and lives."

"Ok...if you say so," Buttons reluctantly answered.

The door to the room they were in opened and a short nervous man in a suit quickly shuffled in. Bubbles and Buttons looked up at the awkward sight.

"You our lawyer," Bubbles asked in disbelief.

"Technically yes and no," the little man answered.

"Huh...what the fuck is that supposed to mean," Bubbles asked.

"It means I am a state appointed attorney but there's nothing I can do to help you two."

"So if you can't help us why don't we have a lawyer who can," Buttons said.

"There is no one that can help you. I

was sent here only as a messenger."

"A messenger...for who," Bubbles asked.

The man pulled out a cell phone, dialed a number and put it on speaker. When the line picked up, a familiar voice answered, "Hello."

"Marco, you son of a bitch, what have you done?!" Bubbles barked.

"Hahaha....I've done nothing but inform a few people about your recent activities."

"You made us fight and kill those women, so you're just as guilty as we are," Buttons angrily voiced.

"Me guilty...my fingerprints are not all over dead bodies and murder weapons and there is a video of you killing my friend Andre so what exactly am I guilty of?"

"YOU'RE NOT GOING TO GET AWAY WITH THIS MARCO, I PROMISE YOU THAT," Bubbles viciously yelled.

"No...you are not going to get away with this. I am here to give you two a choice...either return to Russia to face your crimes here or spend the rest of your life in prison there."

"You can't do this to us Marco! You going to really let him do this to us?! What happened to the American justice system," Bubbles frantically said.

"You have fulfilled your duties sir... they have made their decision to stay and I have no more to say to them." The phone then went silent.

"Sir, sir...he must have hung up. All I can say ma'am is that you two pissed off the wrong people and there's nothing anyone can do to help you."

The attorney went to the door, knocked and quickly disappeared behind it just as he had appeared.

****

Bubbles and Buttons were told they would have to wait at least three years for a trial. Fortunately for them, their time in Russia made them fierce warriors and they quickly dominated the female inmate population. Two years in they became so powerful and dangerous they were put into solitary confinement. After a year in solitary they were finally told they were getting a trial.

When their trial date finally arrived, they were escorted to a cargo van and shackled in to be transported to the federal court house. There were two guards driving them and as they drove a few miles from the prison the driver stun gunned the guard in the passenger seat and incapacitated him.

"What the fuck is going on," Bubbles asked the guard driving. The guard just drove without responding until he reached South Florida. He then drove to a motel called the Outbound Motel.

He got out of the van and walked over to a car parked in the lot with two men inside. The passenger of the car got out with a black gym bag, handing it to the guard. The guy then jumped into the driver seat of the van while the guard went to the passenger area of the van where Bubbles and Buttons was.

"Please don't kill us sir....if you let us go we promise we will disappear and say nothing to anyone," Buttons pleaded with the guard.

The guard gave Buttons a sideways look then released her and Buttons from their shackles. Stunned and apprehensive by the guards actions, they sat frozen to their seats. The guard then pulled his weapon from his side.

"Get out the van quickly!" There was genuine urgency in this man voice.

The guard spoke English but with a strong accent. Hearing his voice raised the hair on the back of their necks from the thought of the guard being one of Marco's assassins finally exacting his revenge upon them. They were reluctant to follow his orders until he made them a second time but more forceful.

"I said get out of the van now!"

"Okay, okay," Bubbles said as she moved and Buttons followed behind her. When they exited the van, the guy in the drivers seat immediately took off. The guard then handed them a motel room key, the black gym bag and his weapon. They took the key and the gym bag but they hesitated with the weapon.

"Look here... if you're going to kill us then fucking get it over with. I'm getting tired of these goddamn games," Bubbles blurted out in frustration.

"If you don't want it then it's fine with me," the guard answered as he turned to walk away.

"Give it to me," Buttons said to him.

The guard cracked a slight smile,

handed Buttons the weapon went to the other vehicle, driving away.

"What...the...hell...just...happened?!" Buttons asked Bubbles.

"I don't know but I believe we're going to find out in this room," Bubbles responded as she held up the motel room key. When Bubbles opened the gym bag, her eyes bucked, inside was a lot of money and passports.

"What's in there?" Buttons asked. Bubbles showed her what was in the bag and her reaction was the same as Bubbles'.

"If they wanted to kill us, why would they give us all of this..."

"I don't know, let's just go to the room and see what else awaits us," Bubbles replied.

They went to the room, slowly put the

the key in the door and when it unlocked
they cautiously walked into a neat, clean,
empty and air conditioned haven from the
sweltering Florida heat. Buttons hurried
into the room and laid out on the bed.

"Is it finally over... are we finally
free?" Buttons asked cautiously.

"It seems like it for now," Bubbles
responded.

****

Later on that night, out of sight of
prying eyes, they decided to go into town.
They went out to eat and do a little
shopping, still cautious, even though they
were not in Russia or prison. They were,
however, in Leo's old stomping grounds
and they definitely didn't want to get the
attention of his mob associates wanting

answers about his death. As they went from place to place, Buttons thought she noticed a man stalking them but kept quiet, not wanting to alarm Bubbles over nothing.

To test her suspicions, Buttons told Bubbles she had to use the bathroom. Now since they were a few blocks from the hotel, she pointed out a diner where she could go to relieve herself. When they went into the diner, she told Bubbles of her suspicions and had her sit at a corner table watching for the guy as she walked to the bathroom. Just as Buttons said, a man crept into the diner after them. Buttons walked out of the bathroom and they left the diner, lying in wait for their shadow to exit the restaurant.

Just as they expected, the guy exited

the diner shortly after they did. He looked around for them and started to slowly walk.

"He obviously wants to meet us so let's go and give him what he want," Bubbles whispered to Buttons.

As the guy slowly walked looking around for signs of them, they ducked behind cars following him, and at the right moment, they quickly walked up to him face to and Bubbles popped him in the head with a pistol...

Uughh.... What the hell happened? " Joe mumbled as he slowly opened his eyes and struggled to regain his senses.

As Joe became aware of his situation,

he realized he was in a strange room bound to a chair with ropes and completely naked. Joe slowly surveyed the room in hopes of getting some clue as to where he was,   how he ended up here and why he was here.

Due to Joe's position in the room, he was able to see out a window through a fold at the edge of the curtain. Joe struggled to focus his eyes on the outside environment until he saw a large red and green neon sign that read "**Outbound Motel**."

"Outbound Motel... how the fuck did I end up here!" Joe voiced.

From Joe's last memory, he had just left a diner in south Florida where he had been approached by two unknown women... then everything went black.

Joe, Bubbles and Buttons

Maybe that encounter was the beginning of his journey to that motel or maybe that was some sort of dream sequence, Joe thought, until the bathroom door opened.

As the door suddenly opened, Joe's dream sequence quickly became a real life situation with him now being face-to-face with one of the women from his memory and boy was she a sight for sore eyes.

Along with her too being completely naked, from her feet to her neck she was a lucky man's sexual delight but, unfortunately, her face, her only flaw, soured her voluptuous frame. She stood about six feet something and was thick in all the right places...thighs, hips, ass and beasts. Her face though, on the sour note, was covered by more craters than the surface of the moon. It was covered in multiple cuts, scars and bruises, evident of a violent life.

Besides her weathered face, the only thing preventing Joe from obtaining an immediate hard-on was uncertainty and fear of what had happened to him and what was *about* to happen to him.

"You finally awake, huh, mystery man", she asked Joe as she slowly approached him."Now why exactly were you following us? "

Joe laughed, "that's an interesting story... you want to hear it? "

"A story ok.... I'm not going to kill you anyways until Bubbles gets back from the store."

"That sounds fair...ever since two bad ass bitches killed my uncle three years ago, I tried to change my life to one of nonviolence, unfortunately another uncle of mine thought otherwise and tried to kill me. He tried to force me improve my father's fight formula but I refused..."

Buttons wrapped her towel around her waist and sat on the bed, "fight formula... what is that?"

My father was a scientist and our family was kidnapped by the Russian mob. They forced my father to make a super drug to dominate the prison drug market. Unfortunately, when prisoners with heroine in their system took the drug they became very violent, especially, women..."

The guy paused her for emphasis then continued his story...

"Seeing that the women were more dangerous than the men, they created a women's fight league. After they had the formula, they killed my mom and dad but didn't want to kill a child...plus, I knew how my father's formula worked because I helped him often in the laboratory, so they sent me to work for this mob boss..."

Buttons bolted up in the bed!

"Did you say Mob boss?"

"Yea Buttons, you know who I'm talking about..." Joe smiled at her.

Buttons' face became flushed, she jumped off the bed and dropped her towel, stunned, as if she'd seen a ghost...

"Joe?"

"Yeah... it's me," he replied.

There was a slight pause because at this point she didn't know if he was there to be with her or kill her. Her mind told her to be cautious but her heart simply wanted to let go and love him. Buttons decided to follow her heart so she freed Joe from his bindings and and embraced him tenderly with a hug and kiss.

"I missed you," Joe said, holding her close.

"I missed you too baby... did you come here for me?"

"After Marco tried to kill me, I wanted to find the only person I could trust and that is you." He stated honestly.

"I'm here for you Joe. So what are you going to do now, hide out with us? "

"Yes and no. I helped you get out of prison with the help of some connections I made through Marco's business..."

"They won't tell Marco where you are?"She asked this question with obvious concern.

"My formula made them very rich

also and they didn't like the fact that Marco tried to kill me so they're with me. Marco and I had an argument over improving the formula and he blurted out that's the reason he killed my father and mother. For years he had me believing my parents abandoned me. I did my own research and found out Marco and Andre were my uncles. One of Marco's board members, who was close to my uncle Andre, told me the truth and half of the board is behind me... I'm hoping you will be too."

"You know Bubbles and I have your back baby...what do you want us to do?"

"We're going back to kill Marco. What happens after that... we will cross that bridge when we get to it," Joe replied with serious intent.

Buttons gave Joe his clothes and just as he began to dressed Bubbles returned to the room.

"WHY THE FUCK IS HE LOOSE AND GETTING DRESSED," Bubbles yelled so loud, the volume on the TV in the next room lowered noticeably.

Bubbles pulled the pistol the guard had given them, pointing it at Joe.

"Sit yo ass back in that chair before I blow your muthafuckin head off. "

Buttons jumped in between them..

"No wait Bubbles... it's Joe. He came back for us."

"Joe," Bubbles repeated. "Joe...what the fuck are you doing here? "

"Getting you out of prison first of all," Joe answered.

"That was you...thanks Joe," Bubbles

said as she lowered the pistol and walked to Joe, giving him a hug.

"No problem we're family. Now to answer your question. After Marco tried to kill me, I escaped from him so that I can get enough support to return and kill him...Buttons is with me... are you?"

"Hell Yeah I'm with you! I been wanting to kill his ass for some years now," Bubbles responded, a hint of the old blood lust returning in her voice.

"I have a flight out scheduled for tonight and some of my people will be waiting for us in Russia to take us to a safe house."

As they talked there was a knock at the door. Not expecting anyone Bubbles and Buttons froze while Joe went to the door and looked out the peephole. A big smile then came across his face and he quickly opened the door. When he moved aside, the guard that helped them escape walked in, also giving Joe a hug.

"This is my friend Sergio. I know you remember him, he helped you escape."

"Yes we remember him....thank you very much Sergio," Bubbles said, offering her hand...

Sergio then said something to Joe in Russian and Joe responded nodding his head towards Bubbles. The guy then quickly pulled a silenced pistol from his pocket and shoot Bubbles point blank in the head before she could even register what was happening.

"OH...MY...GOD... WHAT THE FUCK WAS THAT JOE!!!"

Buttons screamed as she watched her

long time friend's lifeless body hit the floor.

"Sergio is my cousin and poor Andre was his father. He deserved his revenge after his innocent father was killed, don't you think..."

THE END
OR IS IT???

About The Author

Benjamin J. Patterson was born in New Orleans, Louisiana and discovered his talent and love for writing in an unorthodox manner.

While living in New Orleans during hurricane Katrina, he like many others, went through a horrible ordeal. As a stress reliever he wrote about the things on his mind and from that experience,his first book ***Stuff Happens*** was born. This is his second book and his fledgling flight into fiction.

Author Benjamin J. Patterson

Acknowledgment

First and foremost, I want to thank
God for his continuous guidance and
blessings.
Many thanks also go out to
Kim Morrow, the entire BRPP family
and those who I love for standing
behind and encouraging me.

Books by Benjamin

Stuff Happens